# THE
# LOST
# RAINFOREST

## RUMI'S RIDDLE

ALSO BY ELIOT SCHREFER

*The Lost Rainforest #1: Mez's Magic*
*The Lost Rainforest #2: Gogi's Gambit*

# THE
# LOST
# RAINFOREST

## RUMI'S RIDDLE

# ELIOT SCHREFER

KATHERINE TEGEN BOOKS
An Imprint of HarperCollins Publishers

Katherine Tegen Books is an imprint of HarperCollins Publishers.

The Lost Rainforest #3: Rumi's Riddle
Copyright © 2020 by HarperCollins
www.harpercollinschildrens.com

ISBN 978-0-06-249120-6

Typography by Carla Weise
19 20 21 22 23  PC/LSCH  10 9 8 7 6 5 4 3 2 1
❖
First Edition

*For Wesley and Harper and Henry*

*Excerpt from*
# THE SONG OF THE FIVE
*Verse Three*
*(Translated from the original*
*Ant by Rumi Mosquitoswallow)*

No rest for the five shadowwalkers
chosen by fate
to bear the magic of the eclipse.

Our queen had perished
[. . . but her magic had not.]
[. . . but her plans had not.]

We labored, a body without a brain . . .
. . . and no less intelligent for it.

Tirelessly, we burrowed and dug
burrowed and dug
burrowed and dug
to release
what has always been buried beneath
what has always frothed and bubbled
Magma, the destroyer.

When it erupts, only one animal in a million will survive.
The arithmetic is easy.
One animal in a million
. . . is probably an ant.

# THE
# LOST
# RAINFOREST

## RUMI'S RIDDLE

S MOKE.

Whorls and plumes of smoke.

Rumi stares into the vortex, tapping a suction-cupped finger against his lips. *To get so much particulate matter airborne, the temperature of the heat source must be higher than the surrounding—*

"Rumi, *move!*" Mez cries as she streaks through the moonlit clearing.

Mez sounds fully panicked, which makes it all the stranger that they are, oddly enough, racing *toward* the smoke rather than away from it. Rumi knows that's the plan, Rumi's the one who *came up with* the plan, but Mez's panic reminds Rumi how foolish it is to head right into danger, when every instinct—

"Rumi, *faster*!" It's Gogi this time. A tail whips out to pick up Rumi, and he's suddenly in one of his favorite positions, right on top of a capuchin monkey head, fingers threading through tufts of eyebrow fur. He and Gogi slalom through the treetops, hand over hand and foot over foot, rising and falling through the canopy. Capuchin monkey is the best way to travel. "Thanks for the ride, Gogi."

"No problem," Gogi says, breathing in bursts from the exertion. "Literally. You're about as heavy as a palm nut."

"I'm even liiiiiighter," Lima trills from the sky above.

"Not everything has to be a competition," Rumi grumbles under his breath. Gogi's weaving through the trees starts to make him nauseated, so Rumi closes his eyes and uses hearing more than vision to track their progress. While Lima chirps away above, the panther sisters, Mez and Chumba, slink through the jungle off to one side, only audible because they're moving at such breakneck speed; Sky soars above, making excited caws against the night sky; and finally Banu the sloth is somewhere behind, still within earshot but falling farther into the distance. Banu was the one who volunteered to "take rear guard," and they all agreed that he would join them at the ruins of the Ziggurat of the Sun and Moon once he was able to get there. It wasn't an option for the whole group to slow down to sloth speed, not with the volcano preparing to erupt.

Their strangest companion is Auriel.

While Gogi makes his way through the treetops, Rumi peers down at the monkey's right foot, where he's clenching what might appear to an unschooled observer to be a slender yellow vine. The shadowwalkers know, though, that it's the reincarnated form of what was once the second-greatest enemy Caldera has ever known. After taking his revenge on the Ant Queen and destroying her for good, Auriel's been reborn a fraction of his old size.

This was all foretold at the Cave of Riddles, of course. But it doesn't make it any less strange to see this curious mute baby snake, looking out at the jungles of Caldera passing by as if he's never seen them before.

What is going through Auriel's mind?

Will he grow bigger?

It seems unwise to bring Auriel anywhere. But, Rumi reasons for the thousandth time, it would be folly *not* to bring him along. He just saved Caldera—maybe he could do it again.

If he doesn't destroy it.

Rumi digs his fingers into the moist skin of his leg, to distract himself from the compulsive loop of his thoughts. The volcano under their rainforest hasn't erupted yet, but its rumblings are accelerating. By this pace it will be eight nights before there's no space at all between them, which he can only assume means the volcano will be going off. An exploding volcano—can any creature alive in Caldera help against that?

Auriel seems to think so. Soon after the defeat of the Ant Queen, he had waited until all the shadowwalkers' attention was on him, then slithered around in the dirt until he'd drawn a surprising likeness of a volcano cropping up out of the water. Then he'd reared back and smashed it all. Then he'd gone back to staring at them expectantly.

Rumi was the one to point out that perhaps Auriel meant to stop the volcano. It was all they had to go on.

Granted, it wasn't much. *Think, Rumi, think! A better answer is always out there!*

There's a nagging feeling in his mind, and he realizes it's guilt. Emotions are always that way for Rumi; he'll feel a thing and only figure out what it really is after pondering it for a long time. He's let his friends down, that's it. Rumi's usually the one to come up with the big plans—though Sky's done his part, too—but here he is, racking his brain and turning up nothing. A mind seems such a puny thing against the power of a volcano. Surely journeying to the site of the eruption is a reasonable start. But what happens once they get there? What use is something as insubstantial as strategy against a million tons of magma? They'll just put Auriel near it and hope he has some miracle to work?

Wait. Is it actually a *billion* tons of magma? Rumi starts doing calculations to refine his estimate, then stops when he realizes he's distracting himself from his worst concern.

He's got only eight nights to figure out how to stop the volcano.

The reactions of the other rainforest inhabitants confirm the scale of the menace. First it was the pack of capybaras they encountered, braying nervously in the night air as they weaved along a riverbank, keeping their little ones protected in the center of the herd. Soon after were the peccaries, snorting and snuffling as they raced along narrow forest paths, fear revealing the whites of their eyes. Then birds soared overhead, a mix of blue macaws and white egrets and piping plovers, flocks of animals that never flocked together before.

All of them, capybaras and peccaries and birds, were heading in one direction: away from the smoke.

The shadowwalkers are the only ones going toward it.

It's not thick enough to cause trouble for his friends, but Rumi can already sense the acrid smoke on his skin, sharp against his pores. Amphibian problems. He'll have to rig up some kind of mud mask before they get closer to the volcano. He's confident he'll deduce some way to protect his tender skin; that's not the real worry. The real worry is that all the combined brainpower and intuition of the other residents of Caldera is telling them to flee for their lives, and yet Rumi has convinced his fellow shadowwalkers to head straight for the volcano.

He appears to have suggested an unwise course, indeed.

Rumi hears a tree rat scrambling through the canopy. He calls out to it as they cross paths. "What do you know, rat friend?"

"You're heading into danger!" the rat gasps as it races past, bounding up a trunk and leaping to the next branch over. "Go the other way, idiots!"

Then the rat's gone.

"Did you hear that?" Rumi chirps to Gogi.

"Yes. Doesn't exactly inspire confidence," Gogi says, pausing for a moment to catch his breath. He wipes the sweat from his neck and rubs his tired eyes.

Rumi snuggles into the warmth of Gogi's forehead fur, trying to scour the painful smoke residue from his skin. "I'm not feeling especially confident either right now."

"Buddy, I'm thinking, maybe it's best if we join the other animals and get as far away from that smoke as possible. We can't help anyone if we jump right into danger—"

"—and incinerate ourselves," Rumi finishes. "I know. Maybe discretion *is* the better part of valor."

"We are *not* giving up!" Mez calls from the darkness below.

"Yeah!" Chumba adds.

"Just when you think you're out of earshot, panthers impress you all over again. They have simply *amazing* hearing," Rumi admires, his spirits lifting.

"A little too amazing, if you ask me," Gogi grumbles.

"Enough resting, Gogi. Let's get moving!" Mez yells.

"Come on, guys," Lima calls from above, "let's go— hey! Mrph! How rude!" Her voice trails off.

"Lima, are you okay?" Rumi calls up.

"Yeah," she eventually responds. "I flew into a cloud of bats, and I tried to say hello, but they didn't even take the time to answer! Unbelievable. I don't know what's happened to chiropteran manners. I guess imminent doom is making them impolite. Ow, hey! There's another one! Shame on you!"

"They're scared, Lima," Gogi calls up to her. He lowers his voice to a mutter. "Maybe we could take a note from them."

"This is why I spent that year with panthers instead

of my home colony," Lima prattles on indignantly. "You'd think that mighty carnivores would be inferior company to my own kind, but no, bats are basically the worst. I'm much better as an honorary panther. Maybe I can be an honorary capuchin monkey too. Or a tree frog. Or a macaw. Sorry, guys, didn't meant to leave you out. I'm equal-honorary."

"We've been going at breakneck speed for hours," Rumi whispers into Gogi's ear. "How does she have enough breath left over for all this chatter?"

". . . why, hello there, Madame Owl, thank you for finally paying attention to me—wait, *owl*! Ack! Scary!"

Suddenly, with a crashing of branches, Lima is huddling next to Rumi on top of Gogi's head. "I could have been owl meat! I'm traveling down with you guys from here on out."

"Um, my head is starting to feel a little crowded," Gogi says. He holds up his foot, where a skinny yellow snake is writhing. "I've got this stowaway to carry around too, of course."

Owl forgotten, Lima darts her wings forward and plucks up Auriel, draping him across her shoulders. He doesn't seem to mind at all, looping himself loosely around her neck. "How do I look?" Lima asks, twirling around to show off all sides. "Glamorous? Do you like my boa?"

"Very nice," Rumi says. "But I'm not sure if you should . . . I mean, he *is* still a constrictor."

"Aw, he's so little, though! And resurrected Auriel wouldn't hurt me, would you, my handsome reptile friend?"

He stares at her.

"I mean, it's not like you even *could* hurt me, not when you're so small . . . right?" Lima seems suddenly less sure about what Auriel's thinking. She returns him to Gogi's foot. "I'll let you hold on to him after all, I think," she says.

"Good idea," Gogi says.

"Enough resting!" Mez calls up. "We have to cover more ground before the Veil lifts!"

"She's such a taskmaster," Gogi grumbles.

"Yes I am!" Mez calls. "Now get going."

"Yeah!" Chumba echoes.

"What's worse than a panther taskmaster?" Rumi asks.

"Two panther taskmasters," Gogi replies, giving Rumi a high five. Then he sighs, grips a branch with his tail to steady himself, and leaps. Like that, they've lurched into motion, making their way against streams of fleeing animals.

The distant volcano sets the ground rumbling, shaking the nearby branches and sending the smaller animals of the canopy—beetles and mantises and a few unlucky snakes—tumbling to the floor. Rumi scrunches his eyes shut when the vibrations get especially bad. Even though he's clutching Gogi with four suction-cupped limbs, he still nearly loses his grip and tumbles to the jungle floor.

"Is it over yet?" Rumi asks, digging his fingers and toes even deeper into Gogi's wiry fur. In stressful moments like this, he has to focus on stopping the pores on his back from exuding poison. Over the years it's gotten easier, sort of like holding in a sneeze, but he can't afford to get one of the most powerful toxins in the animal world onto Gogi's fur. That would definitely not be a good idea.

Once the rumbling stops, they continue on, more cautiously this time. The sky is ripening, black turning blue at the horizon. "How are you doing, Chumba?" Rumi chirps down after the companions' next pause.

"My daycoma's near," she calls up. "We'll need to find someplace to camp soon."

"I'm on it," Sky calls from above. "I've scouted a spot for us, and have already alerted Banu, so he'll meet us there. Go around the ironwood tree ahead, then follow the trickling stream after. I'll guide you once you're close."

They do as Sky directs, moving downstream to a swampy forested area, then turning a corner to find a den formed by an overhanging rock. Gogi slowly descends his tree until he's right above it. Six eyes blink as monkey, frog, and bat peer into the darkness.

Mez stops short in front of the entrance. "There are panthers here."

"There *were* panthers here," Sky corrects as he crashes through the canopy to the cave opening. The macaw never was one for elegant entrances. Head tilted, he struts into the den, steps one way and then the other. "It's empty now," he caws back. "I saw the panthers fleeing the other way and tracked their path to their home cave here."

"Abandoned," Mez says grimly. "Panthers don't leave a den without a good reason."

Chumba sniffs around the entrance, teeth bared. "It doesn't feel right to enter another panther family's cave."

"I know," Mez says. "But Sky's right, this is the most defensible spot around."

"We're going to defend ourselves from molten lava now?" Gogi says dryly. "Want to tell me how that works?"

"Hello?" Chumba calls out as she heads in.

"Smells like cat pee," Lima says as she flutters into the den.

"It's called *territorial marking*," Mez says.

"Definitely cat pee," Gogi says as he huddles in. "But at least this den is dry."

Lima goes about straightening the den, tossing brittle bones and tufts of rodent fur over her shoulder. "Are you talking about the pee or the rain? Because I think we all assumed the pee would be dry, just smelly. But it will definitely be good to get out of the rain. It doesn't smell too bad in here, I don't think, I'm already used to it, I guess, have you ever smelled bat pee? It's ten times worse, and I'm a bat, which means I'm probably partway immune to it. Or attuned to it? What's the right word here?"

No one answers, but Lima doesn't seem to notice, prattling on as she flits about the dark cave, checking out each corner. Mez and Chumba hole up in one end, tails low, bobbing their noses as they sniff the stale panther scents. Gogi rubs a section of stone clear of cat hair and then daintily places his butt on it, Sky perching on a branch above him.

Rumi gives himself a bath in a mossy, algae-clogged puddle just outside the den, rubbing chilly goopy sludge up and down his arms to neutralize the sting of the ashy air. It feels amazing.

"Looks like you're enjoying that," Gogi says to him. "I don't think I'd feel the same way."

"Here, try," Lima says, picking up a glob of green

sludge and hurling it at Gogi. It misses, striking the cave wall and dribbling to the ground.

"Not funny," Gogi huffs, an uncharacteristic scowl on his face.

Lima's round ears droop. "I was just kidding."

"We've been awake for too long, and in very stressful circumstances," Rumi says, blinking his wide, inky eyes. "I think we could use a sleep. You all can go first. I'll take watch. We amphibians don't need as much uninterrupted sleep as birds and mammals do."

"Is that true?" Lima asks. "I had no idea!"

"Yes," Rumi says, blinking, "it's quite true."

Mez yawns, exposing her set of powerful teeth. "I'd love to rest, but I won't be relaxed enough for a while yet. First we need answers about what exactly went down at the Cave of Riddles."

"Yeah, no sleep until we hear the truth!" Gogi adds, jabbing a finger toward Rumi and Sky.

Soft snoring. Lima's already upside down, eyes closed, narrow rib cage rising and falling evenly.

Gogi nudges her, and she snorts awake. "Yes, yes, I'm up, what's going on? Let's go!" she says as she bursts into the air.

"No, we're not moving," Rumi says gently. "Sky and I are about to tell everyone what happened at the Cave of Riddles, in case it helps us solve the problem of how to stop Caldera from, um, exploding in eight nights' time."

Lima takes back her perch, and nods vigorously. "Yes, stopping Caldera from exploding. Very important." Her nodding becomes less vigorous, and then the snoring starts back up.

"Maybe we just fill Lima in after," Mez says. Chumba's snores join Lima's. "And my sister, too."

"Rumi and I have been over this so many times together," Sky says. "It's hard to imagine that there's any part of our time in the cave that might be useful information, that we wouldn't already have considered."

"That's characteristically self-important," Mez growls.

"We should tell them everything, Sky," Rumi says, hopping so he's between panther and macaw. "There's plenty of chance we might have overlooked something."

Sky doesn't reply. He just inclines his head, waiting for Rumi to start.

Mez settles in, sitting up, head upright and alert. With sunlight dawning outside, casting gray rays along the slippery stone floor, Gogi flounces over Mez, draping his body over her back. Though her expression is still stern, Mez begins purring loudly. It's been well established how much she loves snuggling.

For his part, Rumi continues to bathe himself in algae and goop, while Sky takes up a position beside him, ready to add any details that Rumi misses.

Rumi looks at the loving friends before him. He wants to tell them everything, anything that will help save their rainforest world, but all the same he's worried about where his story will lead, what secrets he's about to reveal. Will they still look at him with such affection once his tale is finished? He can hope so, but no matter how prodigious his reasoning brain, it's proved very inaccurate at predicting the ways of the heart.

Ah well. The only cure for his worry is to continue forward, to take the risk and tell his tale.

Rumi sips some puddle water, makes a big croak to clear his throat, then begins his story.

I should start with a confession: Sky and I seemed more confident than we really were when we left. I got on Sky's back and we flew off, then landed out of sight so we could discuss what we were going to do.

This much we knew: If we wanted to keep our rainforest intact, we needed to destroy the Ant Queen. If we wanted to destroy the Ant Queen, we needed the lens. But seeking out a mysterious ancient lens with only the slimmest idea where it was, or if it still even existed, meant we had plenty to worry about.

All we knew was that the Cave of Riddles was in the far north, so that's where we headed. Our flight took us over misty rolling mountains, the black waters of slow rivers of grass, copses of fig and ironwood and willow, wide swamps dotted with scrubby bushes. Much of it was healthy, but we also passed over zones where the Ant Queen's minions had already worked their scheme, devouring whatever animals they came across and converting the remaining vegetation to fungus farms.

Sky and I shared theories about how the various regions of Caldera influenced one another, watching the riot of saplings that emerged from a fallen giant, tracking the bird populations as they shifted from macaws to pipers to herons. I won't bore you guys with all that.

Eventually we came to a beach. That's where you used the tail feather, Gogi, and we were able to communicate and catch up with everyone's progress. Well, I couldn't hear you, but at least you got to see where we were.

Sky and I knew some sort of boundary between ocean and land had to exist, and we had come up with all sorts of theories about what it would look like, but seeing one in person was truly fascinating! To look out at that expanse of water, as seemingly endless as the broadest jungle, only blue and deep, made us both feel so humble and small. What sorts of creatures might live in that water? How giant and how tiny? How peaceful and how aggressive?

Okay, I see you want me to get to the Cave of Riddles. Sorry, sorry, I'm hurrying!

We traveled as far north as we could, and there, just as

the boto said we would, we found a tall cliff, its stones as yellow as a newly broken branch. I chirped for a while at the beauty of it.

Without any warning, Sky stepped right off the top of the cliff, and swooped down over the iron-gray waves before lifting back up toward the sky. At first I thought he just wanted to give us a close view of the ocean, but then I realized he was scanning the cliff for an opening. Sure enough, he found a cavity halfway up.

We managed the landing, Sky's claws scraping on the stone, and fell into a sort of stunned silence. Above us were strange squiggly carvings, like the ones I'd spent the previous year studying on the blocks of the Ziggurat of the Sun and Moon. The two-legs had clearly been involved with this place, too. My theory is that the carved symbols are a written version of what the extinct two-legs spoke to one another.

I started examining as many as I could, seeing which might be similar to anything I had seen at the ruined temple. Some were images I thought I recognized, a sun or a crescent moon. One was a picture that showed a giant ant being attacked on the underside by two-legs wielding fiery sticks, trying to jab them between plates in the insect's armor. The other carvings would take some time to decipher, if I could manage it at all. I wanted to stay until I figured out as many as I could, but Sky was worried about how much time we'd be wasting, with the lunar eclipse—and its opportunity for harnessing the magic of Caldera—coming ever nearer.

We had a debate, didn't we, Sky? About whether to spend time preparing or race right in? We chose to race in.

It would prove to be a fateful choice.

At first we flew, but the Cave of Riddles was narrow and dark, the rock passageway twisting around unexpected turns, so Sky soon had to land. With his dayflyer eyes, he couldn't make out enough detail of where we were heading. I went first, letting out chirps to let him know where I was. Sky walked on his claws. It's not the most elegant way for a macaw to travel, and I could always hear where he was from the noisy skittering of rocks as I hopped along beside him.

At first the air was briny, and the ground was slick and salty from the sea mists. After a few minutes, though, we were deep enough into the cave that the ocean vapors no longer made it in, and instead the air was musty and dry, like we'd just buried our noses in a pile of gravel. The tunnel narrowed, with large chunks of stone jumbled along the floor, so that one of the two-legs, or even you, Mez, would have found it difficult to pass. But it was not so hard for a macaw and definitely not for a tree frog. Being puny has its advantages!

After its narrowest point, the tunnel opened into a broad and dimly lit chamber. There was a small glowing stone at the far end, but it didn't give off enough light to fill the chamber. I couldn't figure out the other light source, but then Sky jerked his beak toward the roof, pointing out that it was covered in translucent stone panels, ribboned with darker veins. It was amazing how the two-legs had carved the stone to such an incredible thinness that it could let light in from above.

This was no natural cave, that was for sure.

Even in the dusty air we could make out another tunnel that continued deeper into the mountain, again lit from above by the thinly carved stone. I hopped toward it, but then Sky nudged me: there were five more tunnels leading off to the center of the chamber, where there was a simple stone sphere on a pedestal.

The two-legs created the Cave of Riddles to prevent the unworthy from finding the magical lens. I figured that choosing the correct exit tunnel must be our first challenge.

Select the wrong one, and the best case would be that we wandered lost through the inner workings of the cliffs. The worst case? We'd meet our ends, killed by whatever horrific traps or guardians the two-legs had put in place.

We examined the tunnel entrances, but there was nothing to distinguish them. Then we examined the simple stone sphere. Around the circumference of the pedestal, Sky discovered small carvings, just visible in the dim light. Six stages of the moon, like this:

Something didn't feel right, but I couldn't figure out what. I racked my brain for memories of the moon. I'm a frog—we're very lunar focused, but even though I've spent so many long nights croaking up to the moon, I still couldn't remember the order of the moon's phases. I was so mad at myself. Why had I never thought to consider noting, night after night, how the moon changed?

We examined the small glowing stone and discovered that it was embedded in a track carved in the rock, running along the edge of the chamber. With some difficulty, Sky used his beak to push the glowing stone along the track, casting changing shadows around the room. Nothing happened even after he'd moved it a few feet, so rather than tire him out needlessly, we took a break to think.

While Sky and I were puzzling everything through, he observed something that proved useful: instead of thinking which image was right, we could ask ourselves which one was wrong. That was when I realized that, since the revolutions of the moon are regular, its phases should go in a reasonable order. One waxing crescent was in the wrong place. I see you all aren't following. Just trust me, and check it out the next few times you're looking at the moon!

But how to use that information?

Sky suddenly cawed out, and instructed me to wait by the entrance tunnel. He asked me to stare at the sphere, at the light that changed on it while he moved the glowing stone. I didn't understand at first, but then I saw the shadows on the sphere's surface move—they represented the phases of the moon!

Sky continued to adjust the light source, and he didn't need to tell me what I was looking for. I urged him on until the shadow on the sphere was the waxing crescent. Then I told him to step back.

At first there was nothing, but then a grinding sound filled the chamber. The sphere quivered and lowered into the floor, leaving an opening in the center.

Sky and I investigated. The opening dropped a few feet before turning sharply into a sideways tunnel. We'd found our way forward.

Without sparing a moment to celebrate our victory, we passed along the dim tunnel. It brought us scrambling high into the cliffs only to descend again, until the air was cool and the light was nearly gone. Half the time I hopped along, and the other half Sky carried me on his back.

We were both suffering. Sky was nearly blinded, but my eyes could see better in the dark. The chill impacts amphibian blood quicker, though, and I was starting to feel worn down and sluggish by the time we reached our next challenge, the second of three.

We came to a column of open space. High above, as high as the tops of the highest tree, was another panel of thin stone that let in traces of light. The bottom was a pool of water, more still than any water I've ever seen. Not a single trickling stream disturbed its gleaming surface, not a single water skimmer danced on it, which was too bad—I'd started to feel a little hungry.

It took my eyes a few moments to adjust to the light, but once they did I noticed the walls. I thought that the stone merely had strange patterns on it, marbling like you sometimes see on the white pebbles by riverbanks. But it wasn't just texture to the stone; it was decoration, and as tall as the tallest ironwood.

The pictures were of strange trees. At least that's what I thought I was seeing. But I soon noticed that these structures were straighter than any tree can be, and perfectly squared off at the top. There were little boxes up and down them, hundreds, and in those boxes I could see two-legs going about their lives—eating, sleeping, talking. It was like a forest of artificial trees, all jumbled one on top of the other, that the two-legs lived in. Most unusual!

Sky and I studied the drawings as best we could in the dim light, trying to get as much information as possible. It was Sky who noticed, off to the side of the forest of rectangular trees, a trail leading to a mountain—a mountain that was giving off smoke. A volcano, like the one under Caldera, the one we're trying to stop now! Perhaps the very same one. The trail led up to it, and there were strange humped animals, with circles at their bottoms instead of feet, traveling in and out of the mountain, right into the volcano. For what purpose, I had no idea. I still don't.

There are two things we discovered in the drawings that I'm still puzzling through, even today. One is that there was a spot on the shallow edge of the mountain, below the tunnel with the humped animals, that was marked with an X. I don't know why. No matter how much Sky and I examined it, we couldn't find anything particularly special about that location.

Another was a large inset picture of what appeared to be a sort of fish egg. It was being squeezed by amorphous appendages so that it pouched out all over, ready to burst. Then, in the next picture over, another hand held a sharpened stick, and came in from the side to puncture the glob.

In the final picture, the contents of the fish egg spilled

off to the side, the egg emptying. Even an egg-eating frog knows it's cruel to puncture an egg and waste the contents—I still don't know why the two-legs wanted to immortalize such barbarity.

Once we'd finished examining the drawings for as long as we dared, we turned our attention to the smooth gray surface of the pool at the bottom. I'd just asked Sky if he thought we should swim in when the water began to ripple, and a strange creature rose up from the surface. It was long and thin, like a snake, but had gills that flared behind its head, like a fish. It was only about twice as long as I am. Nothing I'd want to eat, but nothing that would want to eat me, either. So at least there was that.

It pivoted one way and then the next, and that's when I realized that this fish had no eyes. Where there would have been eyes was a pink pulsating membrane. I don't know how it was sensing the world, but it clearly knew that Sky and I were there. The strange creature dipped under the surface and stilled. Then it burst through the surface right in front of us, suddenly enough that I hopped right into the air, croaking my head off, and Sky squawked backward.

The long fish hovered its head over the water, then began to speak. It had a sort of voice I've never heard before: high-pitched but dignified, all the same. "You have made it this far, and are the first to do so in many years. I am Kalk, the current guardian of the inner challenge of the Cave of Riddles. My children and their children will serve as guardians when my time is done."

"Hello, Kalk, nice to meet you," I said. Sky made an awkward squawk at that, but I don't know what I was supposed to have said.

You might not be surprised that Kalk didn't say, "Nice to meet you" back. He just kept presenting the challenge. "Only those wise enough to use the lens responsibly will be allowed to pass to the next stage. Your challenge is a riddle. Answer it correctly, and I will ask you two more. Answer it incorrectly, and you will have failed and this chamber will flood, drowning you."

I could have told Kalk that I was an amphibian and that it would take a while for me to drown, and that Sky could fly above the surface . . . but the strange fish would be proven right in the long term; we would eventually succumb. I would rather not inspire Kalk to prove he was right, since that would involve the two of us dying and everything. So instead I told him that I understood his words, and that we were ready.

"Only one of you at a time may respond to the riddles," Kalk said. "Who will go first?"

Sky and I didn't have to discuss for long. Riddles and trivia are pet interests of mine. I stepped forward.

"Here is your first question: What grows whenever it shortens?"

The very first riddle, and I was already stuck. I wanted to look back at Sky for help, but who knew what might happen if Kalk decided that we'd cheated. I started to do a structural analysis of the riddles themselves: they'd have to be solvable by any number of animals that might have approached, so it couldn't be specific to any one time or place or environment. A salamander probably had as much chance as a monkey or a bird. So I decided the answers were probably abstract. I considered saying "tension," but that didn't really seem to fit.

That's when I realized the perfect answer.

"Temper!" I said.

"Very good," Kalk said. "You may proceed to the next platform."

With a grinding sound, a stone rose from within the dark and forbidding pool of water. It was a flat and slimy surface, just above the water level. Sky and I hopped over to it. We were a quarter across the watery chasm now.

Kalk swam so he was directly in front of me. I could see right into his white-pink throat as he spoke. "Your second riddle is this: What grows as the body gets sick, finds fertile soil in sorrow, though age too will do the trick?"

"Wow. I'm sorry, could you repeat that?" I asked.

Kalk did. I tapped my lips. Grows in age and sorrow. Hmm.

*This one was easier. I decided my answer. "Wisdom," I said.*

*Kalk paused. Then he nodded. "Very good. You may proceed."*

*Another grinding sound, and another platform raised. We made our way over. Halfway now!*

*"Here is your final riddle," Kalk said. "What is the only cure for regret, easily sought, but hard to get?"*

*I held perfectly still. My throat pouch started to go in and out rapidly, a sure sign of panic. I'd expected these questions to be math problems or logic puzzles. But they were all about virtues. It made sense, I guess, since the two-legs that had set up the cave were trying to make sure the lens only ended up in honorable hands. I'm not nearly as confident about the emotional side of things, though, as you guys know. This question, especially: it felt like there was a blank space in my mind, where this bit of knowledge should easily lie. I started worrying what was wrong with me!*

*Kalk was perfectly patient. There was no time limit for these riddles. But I would only be able to answer once.*

*Sky's feathers rustled as he shifted on the platform beside me. I looked down, and saw what had captured his attention: great spiny eels were arrowing through the water. They were like Kalk but much larger, wicked teeth extending from their mouths. If this platform dropped now, a few bites and it* would all be over. He wouldn't even need to drown us.

The eels made it even harder to think straight. As I panicked, I could feel poison exuding from my pores. "Don't touch me," I said to Sky.

"Why would I touch you?" Sky answered.

"I don't know! Just don't! Is the answer . . . is it . . ." I said. "Is it knowledge?"

Kalk paused. "You are incorrect."

With a horrible grinding sound, the stone dropped toward the water. I tensed my legs, ready to make a desperate spring to safety. "Stop!" Sky squawked. "Let me try!"

The platform ground to a stop. The eels swam a tight circle around us, a frenzy of spines and teeth. We were barely over the water level.

"Very well," Kalk said. "I will allow you your attempt."

His eye on the thrashing eels, Sky wasted no time. "Is the answer . . . forgiveness?"

Kalk spoke. "The only cure for regret, easily sought, but hard to get—that is indeed forgiveness. You are correct."

The stone rose again, Sky and I scrambling to keep our balance. One last platform rose before us.

"You have passed the second challenge," Kalk said. "Your final test—and the lens—await beyond."

The spiny eels dissipated as we hopped onto the last platform and then beyond, to the far side of the watery cavern.

"Thank you, Sky," I said. "If you hadn't known that answer, we'd have been eel food. Forgiveness. Of course."

"I was stuck on the first two, but that answer came to me right away," he said ruefully. "I guess I have forgiveness on the mind, after my mistake of helping Auriel."

I almost said that I had forgiveness on my mind too, but I didn't want Sky to ask me any questions about it. It wriggled deep into my thoughts, the blank space in my mind around forgiveness. Sky had done something horrible by helping Auriel to nearly destroy us, but he was frank about his guilt, instead of banishing it far away. It made me realize how much I was avoiding my own past. Sky had something to teach me. I decided I would ask him more about forgiveness, and how to find it, on the trip home from the lens—if we survived, of course.

I see you're all confused about what I really mean. We'll get to that part of my tale soon, don't worry.

The far side of the watery chasm was almost completely dark, only traces of the mottled light surviving the trip down. It wasn't too hard for a nightwalker like me, but Sky was fully blind. He followed behind me, and I kept chirping so he'd know where to place his claws. I told him not to follow too near, of course, since I didn't want to accidentally poison him. Technically, my toxins need contact with blood, but I didn't want to take any risks. Sky definitely agreed.

It was a clammy, frigid passageway, and though the moist air was great on my porous skin, I was worried about my cold blood, my metabolism slowing down with no way to rev itself back up again. My limbs were getting uncoordinated, and my thoughts were frazzling further and further. Good thing the riddle challenge was over.

"Halt," came a voice in the darkness.

We were in an open space, my chirps echoing against distant rock walls. The voice sounded like it was coming from all around, from the walls itself.

"You seek the lens, and you have made it farther into the Cave of Riddles than any since the extinction of those who created it. Do you understand the power of the item you seek?"

I was about to give a list of precisely what we understood and what we didn't, but Sky spoke first. "No, we do not understand."

The voice warmed. "That is wise to confess. No one, not even the creatures who made the lens, knows the extent of its power. The sun and moon take turns in their dominion over the rainforest, and the lens has the power to combine their energies, doubling the vital force of Caldera and directing it to a single point. It can create life, and it can take it away."

"That is why we are here," I said. "After the eclipse that made us shadowwalkers, the prison that once held the Ant Queen set her loose again, and she is running amok, trying to *return the rainforest to an older era, when it was just insects and plants. We want the lens so that we—"*

*"You need say no more," the voice said. "I am charged with protecting the lens from unworthy hands, but I do not wish to know what you plan to do with it. If either of you should prove worthy, what he chooses to do with the lens is his affair. Though I would caution you—once the Ant Queen has directed her minions to a task, simply destroying her will not make them stop. If you should win the lens, I will finally sleep. I do not want my rest to be hampered by thoughts of the destruction you might wreak."*

*"What do we have to do to prove ourselves to you?" Sky asked.*

*"To pass the cave's first challenge, you had to demonstrate that you knew the cycles of sun and moon that are the mechanism of the eclipse. To pass the second challenge, you had to show that you were aware of the virtues of a true champion. But an intellectual awareness of virtue is not enough. Does one of you have the inner strength to make the right choices with your newfound power? To answer that, we must know your innermost hearts. You must let us inside, let us see your greatest fear. Do not worry that you have a secret or an insecurity—everyone has those. What we need to see is the possibility of courage, despite vulnerability. Does what you fear most dominate you, or is your fear instead a weary companion, something*

you can spend your whole life living beside?"

"How will you test that?" Sky asked.

"Let us touch you. Let us use that link to enter your mind, to know your innermost selves."

I peered into the chamber's dark shadows. "Hmm. Is there any other option?"

"We will undertake your test," Sky said at the same time.

"What are you?" I asked. I was more nervous than I'd have expected to be. My skin pricked. I could feel the tang of my poison exuding on my back.

"We are the future and past; we are timeless but not bodiless. We are not animals, but neither are we gods. You will never see us in the light, but you will feel us. We will reach out now."

"Wait!" I shrieked. "I have poison exuding."

The voice was unmoved. "We are not afraid of your poison, little frog," it said. "Now, relax. Let us in."

Even when we faced certain death fighting Auriel and the Ant Queen, I never felt as afraid as I did then. Letting some strange creature into my mind—it sounded like the worst kind of torture. It felt like doom. If I didn't know that you all were counting on me, I'd have turned and fled.

I held still, wanting to press against Sky for comfort but too scared to hurt him with my poison. I was all alone, shivering as the first velvety touch came. It was like a soft sort of *worm, or maybe a wet dead leaf curling over my head. Not unpleasant, except when I realized that the . . . thing touching me was also probing deep into my mind. That was when I began to shudder.*

*Out of my control, my thoughts went back in time. Not to our time together, not to my time as a frog, but all the way back to my tadpole days. Back to my home swamp.*

No, *I thought.* Don't make me go back there. Anything but that.

RUMI TAKES A deep breath to gird himself, and is about to barrel through the story of his origins, when the ground starts to shake. He dives under Mez's belly while Sky caws and flaps into the air. The space under Mez's belly gets even more crowded when Gogi joins Rumi.

"Get out!" Mez says. "I'm not going to be able to fight whatever that was if I've got a monkey under me."

"What is it?" Gogi cries as the ground continues to shake. Rumi's collected himself enough to hear the rumbling now, a low sound from deep in the rainforest. It's like the sound from the strengthening volcano, but at a different pitch than before.

Sky flies out of the den. Rumi can hear his friend's wingbeats as he takes a perch somewhere above the entrance. "You have to come see this," Sky calls.

"See what?" Chumba says as she slinks out of the entrance, shaking sleep from her ears. "Oh."

"I want to see, I want to see!" Gogi says, barreling out from under Mez.

Rumi holds on to Mez's underside as she creeps out. When his eyes take in the scene, he lets out a low whistling croak.

The Veil dropped while Rumi was telling his tale. Half the sky is starry night, but the other half—in the direction of Caldera's center, where the volcano is located—has filled with black smoke. Great plumes of it rise and spread, filling the sky with an inky haze. The horizon is lined in orange reds, and Rumi realizes that's from fire. The distant rainforest is aflame. He's never imagined such a thing could happen.

Another rumble shakes the earth. The shadowwalkers instinctively fall into combat crouches, but gradually release. This is not an enemy that can be fought.

Another rumble. "It's so loud," Chumba says, wincing, her ears flattened.

Rumi starts counting the time between rumbles, as a place to put his worried thoughts. *Forty, forty-one.*

Rumble.

Wispy and steady, haze invades their clearing. Their sight distance, already short in the jungle, becomes even shorter. "Are we really going to head farther into that black fog?" Gogi asks.

"Hush," Rumi says. "I'm counting. Fifteen, sixteen . . ."

He gets to ninety, and no rumbles. "Maybe the volcano has calmed down," Mez says, tension reducing her voice to a growl.

"It seems to go in phases," Sky says. "Lots of activity, and then it lulls."

"Like, do you think it might quiet down for a few years? That would be nice," Gogi says.

"That seems highly unlikely," Rumi says. "By my calculations, it's still on track to go off seven Veil drops from now."

"I believe you, little buddy." Gogi sighs.

"I guess we keep moving toward the volcano," Mez says. "What other option do we have?"

There's a creaking sound from the den behind them. Mez whirls, claws out.

"What did I miss?" Lima says, yawning as she walks forward on her feet and wingtips.

"Just the impending doom of Caldera," Sky says.

"Okay," Lima says groggily, smacking her lips and looking around, finally comprehending the black clouds on the horizon. "Wait, what? Oh my!"

They assemble at the cave's exit. Mez, Chumba, and Rumi are alert and watchful, Lima and Gogi yawn and scratch at their arm- and wingpits. Rumi listens carefully to their surroundings, trying to detect any enemies. But the volcano's rumbling has stopped. It's only the usual jungle sounds: throbbing insects and chirping birds and the distant roar of howler monkeys. The wisps of smoke that reached them have started to dissipate. But Rumi knows they'll be back—and worse.

The volcanic rumbling seems to have energized Auriel. He's a yellow arrow zipping around the cave exit, tasting the air before zipping back. "Would you look at that?" Gogi says, tightening his woven sack as he approaches Rumi. "Our little Auriel has grown into such an active young snake."

"He's practically glowing," Rumi says as he admires the line of yellow jagging through the dusky clearing.

"Correction: he literally *is* glowing," Sky says between preenings. "He's lighting up the night out there."

"Well, I'll be," Rumi says. "You're right. That's more light than he was producing before, right?"

"Yes," Sky says, "definitely more."

"What do you think that's about?"

"He appears to be growing in power and size,

without needing to eat," Sky says. "And to be investing himself with some sort of magical ability again. That's as much as we can tell from observation so far. I might hypothesize that he's deriving energy from the volcanic energy, but there's not enough evidence to draw any conclusions yet."

"Well put," Rumi says. "Perhaps there's an accretion of the energies of sun and moon that were released when his resurrected form was destroyed, in addition to any energies being released by the volcano. Whatever the cause, I'd postulate that this process will only continue."

"Come on, guys," Gogi says, scratching his armpit. "I didn't follow any of that. Talk normal, please."

"How big do you think Auriel will get?" Mez asks, pushing her neck toward the ground to stretch her forelegs before the night's travel.

"That," Sky says, "is a very good question."

"He'll do for watching, that much is sure," Chumba says.

"Sky is off the watch list, and Auriel is back on," Lima says. "Got it."

As if he's heard them, Auriel stills and lifts his head.

"Um, just kidding?" Lima squeaks while he stares at her.

Auriel glares for a long moment more, then starts off

into the jungle, toward the plumes of black smoke.

"I guess we're moving," Gogi grumbles. "Let's go, everyone!"

As they head out, though, Rumi hears an odd crunching sort of voice: a turtle. No, make that three turtles. They've camped out in front of the abandoned panther cave, heads extending far from their shells as they gawk at the companions. "Are you . . . ?" one of them begins to ask.

"The heroes of legend who defeated the Ant Queen? Why, yes, we are," Gogi says, winking at the assembled reptiles.

"No," says the second turtle, "we meant . . ."

"The saviors of Caldera? Are you looking for the saviors of Caldera?" Lima offers.

"No," says the third. "Actually, we were wondering about . . ."

"The stalwarts who proved their mettle to the guardians of the Cave of Riddles?" Sky asks, feathers puffing.

"Or perhaps you're looking for Lima the Healing Bat, ferocious-er than a piranha, scarier than a cat?"

"No!" says the first. "We're not looking for any of those!"

"Oh, may you stay still and the sun warm you, elders," Rumi says, slipping into cold-blooded honorifics. "Who are you looking for, hardshells?"

"Thank you, polite frog. Is that the resurrected Auriel, Elemental of Light?"

"Wait, you mean to tell me you're looking for *that guy*?" Lima asks, thumbing her wing in Auriel's direction.

"Yes," says the second turtle. "Passed from bird to mammal to reptile, word has spread of the glowing snake born out of the Ant Queen's doom. We have traveled many miles to learn his wisdom. He must stop the black smoke."

Lima reluctantly nods. "I have to admit, Auriel does sound pretty special when you use those kinds of words."

"As you can see, he doesn't have any wisdom to offer," Mez says. "He's totally mute. And pretty puny. So far."

"Still, he appeared at the same time as the volcano began to erupt," the first turtle presses. "That can't be a coincidence—maybe he has some clue to how we can stop it?"

"That seems logical," Rumi says, nodding. "Auriel does seem to have something in mind for stopping the volcano. We just have to survive long enough to get him there. Tell me, have you seen the volcano eruption up close?"

"Yes," says the third turtle. "It destroyed our homeland. Every other creature that could escape in time did.

We're the last of the survivors. Because we're turtles. Shells and all."

Gogi raps on the hard surface of the nearest turtle's shell. "That has always seemed like a really useful thing to have."

"Would you please stop that?" the turtle asks.

Gogi withdraws his hand. "Oh, I'm so sorry!"

"Could we travel with you, and learn what we can from the Elemental of Light?" the turtle continues.

"There's really not much to learn, I promise," Gogi says. "And we're heading back toward the volcano."

"Near, far, it doesn't matter. Nowhere will be safe once the volcano goes off," says the third turtle, wagging its head.

"Let us see Auriel up close, at least," the first turtle says.

"We don't have time for this," Mez says, eyes on the horizon.

But Lima has already carried Auriel over to the turtles. "Isn't he so pretty?" she asks. "Watch, the yellows change as you look at them, that one's like a parakeet beak, that yellow's more like sunshine, but you guys wouldn't know sunshine because you're a nightwalker species of turtle, but it's a really pretty color, I promise. Anyway, I actually licked Auriel before, he doesn't mind, but he doesn't taste sugary like you might think, he just tastes like snake. It's really a shame."

The turtles *ooh* and *aah* at Auriel, their green faces broadening with joy as Lima places him around their necks, one by one.

"He's the key to solving this, I can feel it in my blood," the second turtle says.

"Okay, Lima, definitely time to go now," Mez says.

The turtles look like they'll never finish admiring Auriel, and Rumi wonders how to break the shadow-walkers away from the group of adoring reptiles. But it's Auriel who leads the charge, promptly uncurling from the turtles and streaking into the nighttime jungle. The companions follow after him.

"This is a most unusual development," Rumi says to Sky as they fly over their friends, who are making their way from treetop to treetop, the two panthers and a monkey leaping between branches.

"Yes. Auriel as inspirational figure. Not what I would have expected, either," Sky says. "I'm sorry your story got cut off, by the way. We'll get back to it as soon as we take our next rest, I'm sure."

"Yeah, wait, hold up everyone, Rumi didn't get to finish his story," Lima chirps out.

"No, no, we're all ready to move now. I'll continue

next break," Rumi says hastily.

As the friends progress through the rainforest, Sky and Rumi fly above, scouting out the animals streaming against them, fleeing the black smoke. During the night-time it's possible to imagine all is well in the rainforest, but when Sky and Rumi scout during the day they can see that the flood of refugees is without end, animals of every sort joining a sorry line of misery. A porcupine has had half its quills singed off. A heron lands on one leg, the other curled away, scarred by fire.

"Should we go talk to it and see if we can get some more information?" Rumi shouts into Sky's ear.

"We might have saved the day against the Ant Queen, but we can't count on rumors winning over the animals we meet. We're still a daywalker-nightwalker pair, and you know how most animals feel about those who cross the Veil. I don't think we should risk it unless the whole group is together. The others are too far off in the canopy."

"Yes, I get it," Rumi says. "I just wish animals would be more evolved, you know?"

"Oh, I understand," Sky says. "I've felt that plenty of times. Say, do you think those birds there would be friendly? I've never known little orange songbirds to be anything but friendly, and they're also always full of gossip."

"I'll hide under your wing," Rumi says. "We don't want them to panic, seeing a nightwalker during the day."

Rumi nestles into Sky's armpit as the macaw lands in the treetop. Birds do have a musty scent by the base of their feathers, but at least they don't have the body odor problems that mammals do. Still, he'll be holding his breath as much as he can.

"Hail," Sky says to the songbirds. "How go the skies?"

"Well met," sing the birds as Sky lands beside them. "The breezes are predictable today."

"May they ever be," Sky responds.

Rumi will have to remember to ask Sky more about this formal language later. There are always new bird manners to learn.

Increasingly frantic bird jibber jabber. The songbirds get more and more excited as they speak, their voices getting so high-pitched that it's hard for Rumi's frog ears to understand them.

"Raise a feather to me, and give me a claw," Sky says, waggling his tail, turning in a half circle, and turning back around. "By the plumes of my underside, I will tell you that I'm heading toward the black smoke. Do you know what currents the air that meets me might contain?"

The songbirds cheep shrilly. "Don't do that!" exclaim the birds. "No, no, don't do that! We suggest you don't. Please go the other way." Like Calisto, the shadowwalker trogon the companions once knew, it seems that songbirds never know quite how to finish making a point.

"I understand it's dangerous, but I don't have any other choice," Sky says. "If I must go, do you have any advice?"

"Do not fly. Walk if you must. The winds are hot. Avoid the Elemental of Darkness. Flying is the best way to avoid it. But don't fly. Only if you have to. Better to walk. Unless the Elemental of Darkness is there. Then fly. But it's too hot to fly."

Rumi's head hurts. He can't even tell which songbird is saying what. He wishes Sky would ask them to speak one at a time, but apparently Sky has no trouble understanding the many birds talking over one another. He is a macaw, after all. They're the loudest and talk-over-one-another-iest of them all.

"The Elemental of Darkness," Sky manages to get in. "What's that? I've never heard of it."

"We have not seen it. I have seen it. No you didn't, that was a rock. Was not! It's worse than the Ant Queen. It's not real at all. It's magical. It's just a normal animal. You can find it in the treetops. But it lives on the ground. The nightwalkers worship it. It eats daywalkers. If it's real. It might not be real. We think it's real."

Rumi's headache spreads.

The songbirds suddenly fly off. Rumi pokes his head out from under Sky's pungent wingpit. "Wow. They didn't even say good-bye."

Sky clacks his beak, his version of a shrug. "I'm used to not getting good-byes."

"I'm not," Rumi says hotly, upset more for his friend's sake than his own. "It's rude of them."

"It doesn't matter what we think," Sky says mournfully. "What matters is how they decide to treat us. In any case—this Elemental of Darkness. Do you think it could be what's causing the volcano to threaten to erupt?"

"It's possible," Rumi says darkly. "As if a volcano weren't already danger enough."

"ONE MORE NIGHT's journey, and that should be it," Mez says as the Veil begins to lift. She plops into a thatch of jungle grass, exhausted.

"And four more drops of the Veil until the volcano goes off," Rumi adds.

"So, brain squad," Gogi says, draping his body over Mez's, stretching out his long arms and legs, "you come up with any great plans over the course of the night?"

Sky looks to Rumi, then clacks his beak. "By the end of the next night, we'll be at the volcano's opening, and then we'll, we'll face this Elemental of Darkness if we have to, and then we'll . . . collapse the volcano!"

"Collapse it how?" Chumba asks, yawning despite a loud rumble that shakes the earth.

"Won't the volcano just melt whatever we try to block it up with?" Lima asks.

"And if the source of the problem is the magma you told us about," Mez presses, "what's to prevent it from just erupting out somewhere else?"

"Like when you squeeze a bug," Lima says sagely. "It might goop out one end or the other, but it's going to goop out *somewhere.*"

They all stare at her.

"What?" she asks. "Haven't you guys ever squeezed the goop out of a bug before?"

It reminds Rumi of the fish-egg diagram he saw in the carvings in the Cave of Riddles. But what did it mean? "Anyway, we're still working out the particulars," Rumi says. "Don't worry, we'll come up with something by the time we arrive."

"You don't have much time," Mez says.

"How do you even fight an Elemental of Darkness?" Gogi asks.

While Chumba falls asleep, Sky looks at Rumi questioningly, then whisper-caws to clear his throat. "So, should we continue with our story of the Cave of Riddles?"

"Oh, there's no need," Rumi says. "We told them all the important information. Don't you think?"

Sky gives Rumi a meaningful look, turning his head almost fully sideways as he does, clacking his beak. *No, we didn't.*

Rumi coughs. "Okay, I—"

He breaks off. A branch snaps, not far off through the jungle growth. The companions go still, Mez low on her paws, teeth bared.

"Oh, that's just our daywalker groupies," Lima says. "They leapfrog ahead of us during the day, then camp out waiting for us to arrive during the night. They're probably just waking up again."

"I'm sorry, what did you say? Daywalker groupies?" Sky asks.

"Didn't you notice? The songbirds are sticking near, and the turtles have been following along behind ever since we met them. There's some monkeys and a tapir or two also."

Mez's ears perk. "Don't you think this is information you should have shared?"

"Sorry!" Lima says. "I don't think they mean any harm. It seems like they want to be near Auriel. Sort of like how flying bugs get attracted to anything that's glowing bright."

"The compulsion of these daywalkers to be near

Auriel must be strong indeed," Rumi says, "since following him also means heading toward the source of the explosions."

"Yeah," Gogi says. "This dry wind is starting to freak me out." The capuchin monkey dabs his sweaty brows. Increasingly, each rumble of the ever-closer volcano comes along with an uncomfortably hot breeze. "I know I wouldn't get any closer to the volcano if you all weren't making me. Tell you what, I'll go talk to them. Where do we think they are?"

"I'll go with you," Lima says cheerfully. "I'm too worked up about our inevitable doom to sleep much, anyway."

Monkey and bat head off into the dawn. Mez lowers her head and flicks her ears. "Once Chumba's awake again, you *will* tell us the rest of what went down in the Cave of Riddles, Rumi," she says.

"Yes, of course, Mez," Rumi says. He watches Mez's flanks slow into steady sleep breathing. "Darn," he whispers to Sky. "I was hoping everyone would have forgotten."

"You should be looking forward to telling them," Sky says. "It will be a relief to get it off your chest."

Rumi shakes his head. "It's so awful. They won't even be able to look at me once they know the truth."

Sky holds out a claw and Rumi takes up his

customary rest position, draped over the macaw's hard black talons. Sky pulls his claw back a little, so Rumi is snuggled under his feathers. "I was able to look at you after *I* found out," Sky says softly.

"Yes, but you're special that way," Rumi says. He closes his eyes, enjoying the feel of his friend's smooth feathers against his back. For the first time in a while, he catches a little sleep.

"It's confirmed. Our daywalker followers are here to be near Auriel," Gogi reports at the next Veil dropping, while they rouse Chumba. "They were asking if I would bring them here to see the Elemental of Light in person. I told them I didn't know, of course. Last thing we need is a bunch of Auriel groupies following us around. They're going about Banu's speed, though, so they'll probably fall behind over this night. Banu is catching a ride on one of the turtles, by the way. He says hi!"

"At least we'll get a head start every time the Veil drops," Mez says as she licks the fur between her sister's ears.

"I can't imagine that any groupies who've come to visit Auriel would want to travel all the way to the edge of the volcano," Rumi says.

"I don't know, hope is a powerful motivator," Sky

says. "Even while they're asleep, I can sense great personal sacrifice from these daywalkers. If the existence of Auriel is making them think there's a chance we'll be able to stop the eruption, then maybe it's worth life and wing to see it through for themselves. Heroism isn't limited to us shadowwalkers."

"Fair enough," Gogi says, patting a sleeping parakeet on the head as he moves past it. "I'm not sure how any random daywalkers can help, but we clearly could use all the assistance we can get."

"We're already risking our own necks to investigate the explosions," Mez says. "I hate to see other animals dragged into it."

"I'm with you," says Chumba as they pick their way along. "Let's make sure we reach the volcano by the end of this nighttime, so for their own safety's sake these sleeping pilgrims won't have time to catch up."

"I think it's all pretty fantastic," Lima chirps from above. "How many animals get *followers*? I know they're here for Auriel, not for us, but still we can pretend they're here for Lima the Healing Bat, am I right?"

"Ooh!" Gogi says. "Sing the song again!"

*"Liiiima, the Healing Bat! Ferocious-er than a piranha! Scarier than a cat!"*

"I've been meaning to ask you. Scarier than a cat?" Mez says. "What's so scary about a cat?"

"Are you kidding me?" Gogi asks. "Have you noticed your claws lately?"

Mez extends and retracts the claws of her front paw, then nods. "Okay, I guess I could see how that's pretty scary."

"Not to mention the teeth," Rumi adds. If he keeps his friends on the topic of teeth and daywalker followers, they might not remember to ask him about his worst memory. Even though he knows he should *want* to tell them.

"We really have to come up with a second stanza for your song," Gogi says to Lima.

"Let me help," Sky offers.

"You?" Mez scoffs.

"Why, don't think I have any lyrical skills in me?"

"I don't, actually."

"I'll look forward to proving you wrong," Sky says. "Macaws are very good at songwriting."

"Are you for real right now?" Gogi asks.

"Want me to help you?" Rumi whispers in his ear.

"Yes, please," Sky caw-whispers back. "I'm not sure that macaws really are that good at songwriting. I just want to be helpful for something more than magical divination."

"I get it," Rumi whispers back. "We'll come up with something good, don't worry."

Rumi starts trying to think of words that rhyme with Lima. It's very hard! Schema? Team-a? But it's a helpful place to put his brain, instead of an imminent volcanic explosion.

All thoughts of rhyming Lima's name vanish from his mind, though, when a rumble from up ahead sets the ground quaking. The companions race into the foliage, huddling under fronds and ferns as a boom shudders the ground, followed by a blast of hot air. It wobbles Rumi's vision, sets his skin pricking and sizzling. "Ow, ow, ow," he says, burrowing deep into Sky's flight feathers.

"You okay there, friend?" Sky asks.

"Yes . . . it's really hot on amphibian skin."

The companions creep out of their shelter and look toward the black plumes ahead. Where the ground rises toward the volcanic center of Caldera, the black plumes of smoke are ridged in sparks of flame, orange rising within the whorls of black.

"We're just seeing the inklings of what's to come. If the volcano actually explodes when we're nearer to it . . ." Rumi says.

"You're right," Mez says, nose wrinkling at the waves of heat. "We're foolish to charge right into danger."

"Thank you!" Gogi says. "I'm linked with fire through my magic, and even I can't believe we're heading right for that disaster."

"Interesting," Lima says. "I know you can make fire appear, Gogi, but can you make it go away?"

"Huh!" Gogi says, scratching his belly. "I've never tried."

"That's promising," Rumi says. "Let's explore it. And that's got me thinking—what about Banu? If he were here, we could also try using his water shield to protect us."

"He's probably resting with the daywalker pilgrims," Mez says. "We could go fetch him and get him to catch up."

"It will slow us down a little, I know," Sky says. "But we won't do Caldera any good if we've all been incinerated."

"Raise your hand if you want to be incinerated," Gogi says.

They're all motionless, except for Lima, who raises a wing. She looks at them all, confused, then puts her wing back down. "I think maybe I don't know what 'incinerated' means," she whispers.

"Okay, that decides it," Mez says. "Go get Banu. Hurry!"

Gogi untwines Auriel from around his neck. "Should I go? Can someone else hold on to Auriel if I do?"

If Auriel understands what Gogi is saying, he makes no sign of it. He tilts his head from side to side, looking about the clearing. Rumi hasn't seen him eat anything, but he's growing an inch a night, at least. Maybe he's absorbing the volcanic energies, or the sunshine itself? Or he's absorbing carbon from the air and turning it solid, the way that trees do?

"I think Lima and I will be faster," Sky says.

"You and me?" Lima asks, gulping. Then she nods. "There's a first time for everything. Okay. We'll get Banu here in no time. Last one there is a rotten egg. Sorry, is that offensive to a bird? Anyway, let's race, here we go!"

Lima takes off and Sky follows her, the two flying animals soon disappearing from view. Rumi can still hear Lima's stream of prattle, though. "I think I can take off easier, and adjust my flight more easily, but once you get going, Sky, wow you really can move fast, and it's like you're not using any energy at all, while I, hold on, let me catch my breath, while I have to keep pumping my wings, can we rest yet?" Her voice fades from hearing.

Now that Sky is gone, Rumi feels an ache that he can't quite place.

Gogi notices Rumi's expression, and sits down next to his friend. "This is the first time you and Sky have been apart in a long time, isn't it?"

"I guess it is," Rumi says, nodding.

"He'll be back soon, don't worry," Gogi says, picking

Rumi up and tucking him in the crook of his arm.

"Thanks, Gogi," Rumi says. While they wait, Rumi gives up on trying to rhyme "Lima," and instead times the rumbles, to see if he can come up with any insights there. The volcano will make a few rumbles in a row, then go silent for long periods of time. *Four hundred and ten seconds, four hundred and eleven—there's another one!* If only the rumblings weren't so horrifying, the process of counting would be soothing.

"Hey, Rumi," Gogi whispers, giving him a tap on the head. "You know that whatever you have to say about what came out in the Cave of Riddles, it's going to be okay, right?"

Rumi gulps. "Did Sky already tell you?"

"No, of course not," Gogi says. "But you're avoiding something, and we monkeys are attuned to stuff like that."

"Thanks for saying that." Rumi sighs. "I'll tell you very soon, I promise."

Rumi waits for Gogi to press him further, but his friend just sits there, patting Rumi's head. He blinks his big frog eyes against unexpected tears.

It's not long before Sky and Lima arrive—with Banu. The sloth sprawls out in the nighttime clearing, eyes closed and chest heaving.

"Banu!" Gogi exclaims. "You made it!"

Rumi claps his hands. "You brought him back so quickly!"

"I know!" Lima exclaims, crash-landing on the ground and rolling. She gets back up to her feet, shaking her wings victoriously. "Banu's not so slow anymore!"

"I've been getting . . . faster than I thought I could . . . the fastest . . . a sloth . . . has ever . . . had to travel," Banu pants, dramatically flinging a clawed hand over his face.

"Banu," Rumi says, throat pouch trembling. "You definitely deserve a chance to rest, but unfortunately we have a bit of a crisis. There are hot blasts coming from the volcano, and as we get closer, we're worried that they could get hotter. Soon it will fully go off, too, and then we'll *really* be in trouble."

"—and we would be some very crispy shadowwalkers," Lima adds.

With a great wheezing sigh, Banu sits up. "Okay . . . I think I understand . . . what do you need . . . from me?"

"We need you to leverage your extraordinary powers to mitigate any deleterious thermal effects," Rumi says. "Can you do that?"

Banu blinks.

"Did I misspeak?" Rumi asks.

"What Rumi's asking is: Can you make us a water shield?" Sky asks.

"Oh!" Banu says. "All you had to do . . . is say so. Of course I can . . . happy to . . . not so hard, really." His eyes cross for a moment, and then there's a liquid dome surrounding the companions. Water shimmers all around them, and the starlight diffuses over the surface.

"Wow," Lima says, poking a wing in and out of the shield. "That is so sparkly. I *love* it!"

"It's extraordinary," Rumi says. "But it does seem to create visibility problems."

"Yeah," Mez says, approaching the shimmering boundary and dipping a paw in, then holding it up to her face and licking it. "I can't see a thing through this."

"Right, sorry," Banu says. The dome disappears, leaving just a ring of wet earth.

"Can you conjure it back up quickly?" Rumi asks.

"Yes," Banu explains. "I create it from . . . the water vapor in the air." The dome is instantly back.

"Okay!" Gogi says. "Apparently this will work. We'll move forward with Banu in the center, and he'll throw up the water shield if there's a blast of heat."

"As long as . . . you're willing . . . to move at a sloth's pace."

"Can we make it the fastest sloth's pace that you can manage?" Mez asks. She tries to smile patiently, but it just displays her long canines. Banu's eyes widen in fear.

"So, can you give me a long water tail?" Lima asks.

"Or a water beard? Or, like, a bunch of dewdrops all over my belly that sparkle whenever I move?"

"Not now, Lima," Mez says. "Save the body decorating for when the future of Caldera isn't at stake."

"Fine." Lima sighs.

"To . . . the volcano!" Banu says.

"Let's do this," Mez says, already starting along the path.

As he hops along, Rumi stares up at the column of black smoke. The volcano isn't actively erupting at the moment, but he's kept up his counting during his conversation with his friends. It appears that each explosion can be estimated by $n + 455$, where $n$ represents the time in seconds of the last explosion. Which means that the next explosion should be—

Rumi sees the blast rocketing toward them, certain death bearing down, faster than a swooping eagle. "Banu, shield now!" he cries.

The startled sloth barely has time to raise an eyebrow before the cascade of hot air is upon them, stronger than ever before, laced through with ferocious plumes of smoke and burning embers. Rumi cringes away, but then the hot wind poofs. Banu's raised the water shield, and just in time. With a pop and a crack, the water turns to steam, deflecting the deadly heat up into the air.

Banu scrunches his eyes shut as he increases the thickness of the water shield, pushing against more and more of the ashy volcanic blast. The companions huddle around him, Gogi tucking Lima and Rumi under his chin to keep the most fragile shadowwalkers safe.

"Banu, how long can you keep this up?" Rumi asks. But Banu can't spare any attention, all his energy focused on maintaining the watery barrier. The fizzing and sizzling finally quiet, though, and Rumi gives the sloth a tap on the head. "I think we're good for now."

Banu lets the water shield drop. They're surrounded by a ring of healthy wet jungle, but outside the circular boundary, the trees are charred and smoking. The air is clogged with ash. "Wow," Chumba says, covering her mouth with a paw. "A volcano is no joke."

"It's not even in full eruption mode," Rumi says. "This is really just premonitions of future activity."

"I'd rather not see *that* up close," Chumba says.

"Yes," Sky says gravely. "That's why we're doing all this. To stop anyone from seeing the eruption up close."

"Banu, could you move us a few dozen panther-lengths toward the volcano? I think I see something I recognize."

They all move as one awkward, nervous lump, everyone pressed as tight as they can to Banu, so they're safe if the volcano sends out another blast.

"Right here," Mez says, sniffing around the ground. "Does anyone else remember this spot?"

Gogi turns around. "Can't say I do. Looks like . . . jungle to me."

"Not even the best sort of jungle," Lima says.

"This is where we came out after we went beneath the ziggurat, long ago, and first saw the Ant Queen in her prison. This is where we escaped!" Mez says.

"So it is!" Rumi exclaims. He runs his fingers through the silky soil. "This is the exact texture of the earth at that spot. Most impressive memory, Mez."

"You think that maybe we can get back down beneath from here?" Sky asks.

"It caved in while we escaped," Mez says. "At the time it looked like a fresh wound in the earth, but it's been a long time now, and the jungle has taken it back over. Just like it's grown over the ziggurat ruins. But if we could move this soil, then we could get back down beneath, and maybe see what we could do about blocking the magma flow heading into the volcano."

"Does anyone believe this is actually going to work?" Gogi asks.

"Of course it will!" Lima says. "We'll, um, create a cave-in! Easy-peasy."

"Yes, something like that," Sky says, nodding.

Chumba, always the most decisive among them, starts digging into the grassy earth with her front paw. "Chumba," Mez says, "that will take forever."

Rumi glances at Sky. "This is why we resurrected Auriel, anyway. Because he has powers over the earth."

"Who, this hefty little guy?" Gogi asks, holding up the length of yellow snake. Somehow, Auriel seems to have grown even more over the last few hours. He's about as long as the capuchin is from head to tail, now, and probably the same weight.

Auriel stares at them.

"In his old form, Auriel absorbed the powers of some of the eclipse-born animals, and one of those was Niko the catfish, may he rest in peace," Sky says. "Niko had the power to move earth. Auriel might still have that potential now."

"Auriel," Lima commands, waving her wing, "open up the earth!"

"I don't think it'll be that easy," Gogi says gently.

Auriel slinks down from Gogi's arms and passes through the grass. He comes to a raw patch of ashy earth and pauses. He noses the soil. Then, without warning, he disappears.

"What the what?" Gogi asks, scrambling after

Auriel. "Where did he just go?"

The ground around them begins to quake. Mez and Chumba and Gogi streak up the nearest tree, and Rumi jumps to Sky's back as he and Lima take to the air. Banu makes it to the nearest trunk and clutches it with his curved claws.

While they watch, the ground funnels down, pouring like water. It continues to rumble and fall, passing into a void below, until it slows and stops.

When the dust settles, Rumi sees that a tunnel has appeared, going only a short way before falling into absolute darkness.

"We're not really going to go in there, are we?" Gogi asks.

"Apparently we are, if Auriel has anything to say about it," Mez says, pointing her ear at the tunnel.

There's a streaking yellow glow, and then Auriel appears, staring at them impassively. He turns around and sidles into the tunnel. His glowing scales illuminate the ragged earth all around, but already the tunnel entrance is darkening as Auriel slithers farther and farther away.

"We should follow before he gets too far. His scales illuminate the passage, which is pretty handy," Rumi says.

"Unless he means to simply collapse it once we're all inside," Mez says. "It would be a brilliant way to do us all in. He wouldn't even have to worry about separate burials."

"Wow, that was super dark, Mez," Gogi says.

"This new Auriel of Light destroyed the Ant Queen, and saved all of Caldera," Sky sniffs. "I think we can assume he means well."

"You've always had a soft spot for that boa constrictor," Mez growls.

"No time for bickering. He's slipping away. If we mean to use the benefit of his light, we have to move now!" Rumi says. Just what does Auriel have in mind?

Lima decides it for them. She arrows after Auriel. "Thank you!" she calls. "You were so obedient. What a well-behaved little snake. Or medium-sized snake now, I guess. Oh, wow, this tunnel is amazing. Wait up!"

Her voice fades as she flits away.

"Here goes," Mez says. She and then Chumba creep into the tunnel, followed by Gogi, who fires up the tip of his tail to provide extra illumination. Sky and Rumi take the rear.

"I'll wait for you guys out here!" Banu calls, cupping his clawed hands around his mouth. "I'm not so good at dodging lava flows."

"Okay, we'll miss your water magic, but safety first!" Rumi calls back, then settles into Sky's wingpit. It's not such a bad way to travel, really.

"I wish there was a place we could have studied more on how to stop a volcano," Rumi says. "The ziggurat carvings had a lot of information from the two-leg civilization locked into them, but none of those dealt with the eruption itself."

"Hold quiet for a moment," Sky squawks. He cocks his head, listening.

Unfortunately, though, up ahead, Lima is maintaining her one-way conversation with Auriel. Sky's eyes flash with irritation.

"Do you hear something?" Rumi asks, dropping from Sky's wingpit and hopping along the tunnelway.

"Hard to tell under Lima's chatter, but it sounds like . . . singing," Sky says.

"Singing! How unexpected."

Lima pauses up ahead. "Anyone else hear that song?"

"Even when she's blabbering," Rumi says, "Lima's got the best hearing of all of us."

"There's singing . . . and steam," Mez's voice reports. "Lots of steam. Rumi, I'm worried about your skin down here."

"Me too," Rumi says. "Thanks, Mez. Sky?"

"Come right in," Sky says. He lifts his wing and

clicks his beak. Rumi hops underneath, and it closes around him. It means missing out on what the companions are seeing, but he's decided he'd rather not be a steamed frog. He wasn't able to make out a great deal of his surroundings in the yellow shadows of Gogi's and Auriel's reflected light, anyway.

Sky's feathers rustle as he continues along the darkened passageway, the noise joining the click of his claws along the stone floor. Hearing the sounds of Sky's awkward walk through the vibrations of his very bones and feathers makes Rumi feel close to his friend.

"Would you look at this?" Mez says up ahead. "Everyone move carefully, the path drops off quickly from here."

Before Rumi can ask him to, Sky narrates what he sees. "We're at the edge of a rocky face, looking down to an empty gap."

"It's where the Ant Queen's prison was, if you remember," Mez adds.

"Oh, I remember," Rumi says, but he has no idea if his words come through the barrier of Sky's feathers.

"I don't think there's any way for the non-flyers among us to get below," Sky continues. "Not that I think any of us would want to. There's magma down there."

"And the singing," Rumi says. "It's louder. Can you make out the words, Lima?"

"I'll go check," Lima says, her voice already fading as she flies off.

Rumi risks poking his head out to look around. It's brighter than he thought it would be, the cavern walls glittering. He cranes his head to see down, and finds a river of molten orange snaking far beneath. It's a thousand frog-lengths off, but still the heat rising from it is almost unbearable. He lets out some breeze from his mouth, only as much as he's able to produce with his limited magic, just enough to keep the air moving. "Magma," he whispers. "We're seeing magma in person. Like we saw depicted in the carvings in the Cave of Riddles."

"You sound almost excited," Sky says.

"I suppose I am. Scared, too, but this is not something that a tree frog like me ever expected to see in his life. My knowledge expands a lot today."

"There's only one of you in this world, you know that?" Sky says.

"Yes, and perhaps it's for the best," Rumi says, sighing.

"I don't know about that. But I'm glad I get to know you." Rumi's eyes water unexpectedly. Praise from someone like Gogi is lovely whenever it happens. From someone like Sky, it's a rarer jewel altogether.

"Thank you," Rumi says as he ducks his head away, back under Sky's protection.

Before Sky can respond, Lima's voice comes trilling through the cavern. "I know who's singing, and you guys aren't going to like it one bit. It's *ants*."

"I'M GOING TO get closer to see if I can hear their weirdo ant words better," Lima says.

Before any of them can stop her, she's flitting through the ruddy light.

"Lima, come back! It's too dangerous," Gogi calls. He's wrapped his tail around an outcropping in the rock, and lowers himself down, hands flailing for Lima.

She's out of reach, though. "Lima, be careful," Mez whispers, extending and retracting her claws against the stone floor.

It's not too long, though, before Lima's back, landing on Gogi's open palm. Sweat mats the black fur on her face, and her skin is red. "Are you okay?" Chumba asks.

"Shh, shh, I'm trying to remember the song. Memory is hard for bats." She taps her forehead, then looks her sweat-covered wing. "You're right, I'm soaked. Anyway, what are the words, what are the words? Oh I remember. 'We are the six-legged poops!' No, that can't be it!"

Lima heads back to the edge, preparing to dive back toward the magma and the ant song.

"No, stop. Gogi, grab her!" Mez cries. Gogi whips out with his tail and captures Lima right as she takes off. He reels the startled bat back in, placing her on the stone.

"Did you really just do that to me?" she cries.

"Shh, Lima, I have another idea," Mez says. "Follow me. We all can listen, and that way we don't have to depend on bat memory."

Mez pads back from the edge, then uses an outcropping as a stepping-stone to descend. She skirts a narrow ledge, and then descends again. "The way is clear, but Chumba, you might want to wait—"

With a few short steps, Chumba is right behind her sister. "—never mind," Mez finishes.

With Rumi holding firmly on to Sky's armpit feathers,

the macaw picks his way down the sheer face of stone, using his beak and claws. Gogi takes up the rear. "Okay, all here," Sky says.

Rumi maneuvers from under Sky's wing so that his head is exposed and his ear has unfettered access to the song rising from below. The dry, blasting heat wrinkles his face, but it's worth the pain to hear the song for himself.

Once he can hear the words, he starts fear-chirping.

*We have a queen no more*
*. . . though we lived with her imprisoned for more*
  *years*
*. . . than there were bricks in the ziggurat.*

*Even without a queen, we are*
*the most powerful animals in the rainforest.*

*We needed her to set our mission,*
*to remind us of the wondrous beginnings of Caldera*
*[ . . . of Earth.]*
*Of a time when there were only ants and plants*
*And there was no such thing as strife*
*Or murder*
*[ . . . or vertebrae.]*

*Our dead queen left us a blunter plan,*
*to burrow beneath the surface of Caldera*
*[Where there are natural forces more powerful than*
*    any animal.]*


*Only rock separates magma*
*from tender animal.*
*A shallow barrier that trillions of mandibles*
*can break.*


"'Earth,'" Rumi says, savoring the unusual word. "What do you suppose 'Earth' means?"

"Definitions don't seem our most important concern at the moment," Sky says.

"Definitions can be crucially important," Rumi huffs.

"Yeah, especially when that 'erupt' thing is the ants' master plan for destroying us all!" Gogi frets.

"So wait, they're speeding up the eruption?" Lima asks.

"Yes, in a blunt way," Sky says, peering down.

"What does that mean, 'blunt'?" Chumba asks. "I can't see anything but magma down there."

"Sorry, I forgot bird eyes can see farther," Sky says. "There's a stream of ants at the edge of the rock, using their mandibles to burrow through. It's slow work, but they're gradually eroding the rock into the magma flow. They're incinerating themselves in the process."

Rumi cranes his neck out, trying to see, but there are too many red flight feathers in the way.

"There will always be more ants," Gogi says.

"So what do we do?" Lima chirps. "By the way, are you guys thirsty? Whew, I could drink a lake right now."

"Lima makes a good point—we shouldn't stay here much longer," Mez pants. "Rumi, are you okay?"

"I'm fine," Rumi says, running his fingers over the skin of his head. It feels waxy, and a headache is blooming behind his eyes. "I think that, once all of this is over, I will do a study of the songs of the ants. They have a most unusual structure, and breaking down how they function might give us clues to the phenomenology of what it is like to be an insect. Given their single voice, it seems like it's almost more apt to call the whole colony a singular organism with satellite parts, instead of individual animals."

"Sure, okay, buddy," Gogi says. "In the meantime, though, do you have any ideas about how we can stop the ants from burrowing into the earth and releasing more magma?"

"Sadly, no," Rumi says. "Back when there was a

queen, there was someone specific for us to rail against. It's like her intelligence has simply been distributed among her minions. But ants outnumber and outweigh us. There's no hope of our defeating them. There was some hope when it was just magma we were fighting against. But now, the only course I can devise is to find some way to escape."

"Escape Caldera?" Gogi asks. "How can we do that, when Caldera is all that there is?"

"That's simply not true," Rumi says. "Sky and I saw the edge, and you saw it with us. Caldera is surrounded by water. Perhaps, on the other side of the water, there is more land."

Lima lets out a low whistle. "Abandon home? You're blowing my mind here."

Heat flashes up from below. "Guys," Chumba pants, "I think we need to get out of here. I'm overheating."

"Let's get a move on," Mez says. "We'll talk more about this crazy idea of yours once we get to the surface, Rumi."

They retreat through the tunnel. The heat has made them sluggish, moving forward with methodical, plodding steps. Even Lima's cheer seems to be flagging. No songs from her anymore.

"How is this possible?" Gogi calls, up ahead.

Sky and Rumi turn a corner to see a wall of stone. Hot dust fills the air, curling Rumi's nose.

"This was not here before," Chumba says.

"No," Mez says, "it definitely wasn't."

"Oh my gosh, oh my gosh," Lima says, her voice rising into an unintelligible squeak at the end.

"One of those rumbles we heard while we were far below must have been this cave-in," Rumi says, turning in circles as he looks for a way out. "The ants are changing this underground landscape so rapidly."

"What do we do?" Sky caws. "It's not like there were any other passageways down here."

"We're not stuck, are we?" Lima chirps, her voice briefly lowering to an intelligible level before squeaking off again.

"Let's try not to panic," Rumi says. Even as he says it, the shadowwalkers are doing just that, bumping into one another in the near darkness, their breaths quick and terrified.

The only one who keeps calm is Auriel. He unfurls from around Gogi's shoulders, his glowing yellow body cascading to the ground. He licks the hot and dusty air, woggles his head one way and then the next.

He holds perfectly still.

Then he leaps!

Rumi would never have thought that a snake could do such a thing. Auriel springs at the wall of rock, glowing ever brighter as he arcs. Once he hits the stone wall, he passes into it like it's a puddle of muddy water, the stone smoothly parting around his body. It doesn't re-form behind him, but splits for good, the splash of Auriel's impact leaving a passageway sloping upward through the rock, wide enough for a panther.

"Go now, everyone," Rumi says, "in case it closes up again!"

While the rest of the companions hang back, girding themselves, Sky is the first to try the sudden passageway, bringing Rumi right along with him. They clamber into the black tunnel, and Rumi risks peeking his head out from Sky's wingpit so his inky black eyes can watch the smooth surface of the passing stone. It's marvelous, reflecting the many radiances that come off Auriel's scales. It's also terrifying, and he has the feeling that at any moment the rock could turn liquid again and drown them all.

Despite his academic interest, Rumi can't wait for this journey through narrow hot rock to be over. He was entombed in rock once, back when he was the Ant Queen's prisoner, and would rather not do it again.

"Are the rest of you getting along okay back there?" Rumi asks, directing his words behind them.

"Mrph, I just want out of here," comes Mez's muffled voice.

"I know the feeling. Just keep pushing through!" Rumi calls back.

Sure enough, the tunnel slopes sharply up, then broadens to show a circle of starry sky. Auriel's glowing body slips into the rainforest, Sky staggering after. Rumi drops out of the wingpit and whirls once he lands, just in time to see two panthers, a monkey, and a very harried-looking bat come after. "Ack, that was awful," Lima says. She taps her nose experimentally with the tip of a wing. "I'm pretty sure all of my mucus crisped away."

"It comes back," Gogi says cheerfully.

"Gross."

"You're the one who brought up snot in the first place, and *I'm* the gross one?"

"Yeah! You are!"

"Look!" Chumba says. The edge in her voice shuts Gogi and Lima right up, bringing their attention to the line of jungle trees.

Auriel has slunk halfway there, and then paused before the looming darkness. A ring of nightwalkers faces them, glowering at the bright yellow snake. These are not like the daywalker admirers. Claws and talons are out. Two owls, a dwarf crocodile, a chinchilla. "Is this the one?" one owl says to the other.

"Yes. The yellow snake. The sworn enemy of the Elemental of Darkness," says the second owl.

"Excuse you!" Lima says hotly. "Auriel is no one's enemy. He just saved us from a stinky hot cave. And he's going to stop this volcano explosion somehow."

"Auriel! That's his name!" trills the chinchilla. "Attack!"

"Lima!" Rumi mutters, shaking his head.

Caught off guard, the companions work to set up their battle positions while the nightwalkers streak toward them. Gogi readies licks of flames at his palms, Mez blinks invisible, and Rumi takes in a big breath, to get as much as he can out of his wind powers.

Rumi assumed Auriel would flee back to the shelter of his allies, but he's holding perfectly still. Auriel is so calm that Rumi goes from being worried about his welfare to worrying about that of the nightwalkers. Although they're attacking the shadowwalkers, it could be over a misunderstanding, and they might lose their lives for it.

Rumi lets out a powerful wind, to slow their enemies.

But all that comes out is a slight breeze.

*What in the world?* Rumi hops forward, hoping

against hope that he'll produce a bigger wind when he tries again.

As the nightwalkers streak toward Auriel, an unexpected ally comes forth.

The line of jungle parts again to reveal a panther, slightly smaller than Mez and Chumba. It races after the nightwalkers.

The new panther reaches the dwarf crocodile first, pouncing onto its backside, raking its claws into the beast's scales as the two go tumbling. Once it's got the ambushed crocodile on its back, the panther bites hard into its belly. The end is quick; the reptile goes still.

Rumi maximizes the surprise generated by their unexpected ally to target a tight cylinder of wind at the owls. It's far weaker than he hoped, and doesn't have much impact on the birds' silent flight. Something is wrong with his power!

Luckily, Gogi had a similar idea, and his fire power doesn't seem to be suffering from the same cramp that's afflicting Rumi. His bolts of flame strike the owls mid-flight, and they go from smoothly soaring to tumbling to either side of the night sky. "Thanks, Gogi!" Rumi cries.

"No problem, buddy," Gogi says. He scans about for the owls, who are now nowhere to be seen. Rumi hangs his head. There's something definitely wrong with him.

With the crocodile dead and the owls pitched off to the side, that leaves only the chinchilla to oppose them. The courageous little rodent approaches Auriel, long front teeth gnashing the air, then seems to realize it's all alone. It looks behind it, then up, then back to Auriel, floppy ears wagging. It wiggles its nose, then turns and bounds into the night.

The only stranger here now is the unfamiliar panther that came to their aid.

"Thank you, friend!" Gogi calls out.

Panting heavily from its assault on the dwarf crocodile, the panther staggers toward them.

"Is that . . ." Mez says.

"It can't be!" Chumba says.

Lima squeaks. "Yerlo?"

"Lima," he says. The exhausted young panther looks at the rest of the companions in turn. "Mez, Chumba! And you must be Rumi and Gogi." Yerlo looks last to the scarlet macaw, head cocked.

"This is Sky," Lima says. "We, um, might have bad talked him when I stayed with you that year, but he's really not such an awful guy."

"Thank you for the lovely introduction," Sky says.

The fronds of a nearby fern fold down. "And I'm Banu . . . I'm often very . . . late to arrive . . . thank you . . . for your help back there."

Yerlo nods, for the moment too exhausted for words. He just stares wide-eyed at Auriel's glowing yellow body. Once he's caught his breath, he speaks again. "And that is really the one? The Elemental of Light?"

"We just call him Auriel, cousin. No need to stand on ceremony," Mez says. Her tail thrashes with worry. "Why are you here? Has something happened at home? Not—the lava?"

Rumi's eyes flit to the night sky. "It sounds like we have a lot to talk about," he says. "Might I suggest we do it somewhere else, where there aren't murderous owls swooping about?"

"Getting away from murderous owls sounds like a good idea," Lima says, shivering as she holds her mouth open to echolocate any enemies. "I can't detect them now, but owls are infamously stealthy."

Mez gives Yerlo a ferocious headbutt, which startles Rumi at first, until he sees Chumba do the same thing and then hears the thick sound of the cats' combined purring. Felines are weird. "Yes," Mez says, "let's get into the underbrush. My cousin and sister will be in daycoma soon, anyway. Whatever the reason, it's good to see you again, Yerlo. I've missed you."

"I've missed you too," Yerlo says, tears in his voice. "You have no idea what's been happening."

Mez nods. "I know you'll tell us as soon as you can."

Chastened, the companions slink off into the brush.

6

MEZ LEADS THEM to the dark hollow of a monguba. It's not a big tree, but the hollow is wide enough to fit them all, bodies slotted one against the next. It's soon hot and sweaty inside, but in Rumi's mind the increased safety is more than worth any discomfort. A warm-blooded animal might have a different opinion, of course. He looks at Gogi inquiringly, but the monkey is busy sizing up Yerlo. Of course—panthers are monkey killers, and though Yerlo almost certainly wouldn't take a bite out of one of his cousin's friends, "almost" doesn't go quite far enough when you're all pressed together into a tight space.

Without needing to discuss it, Gogi, Sky, and Lima

crawl over Mez and Chumba so that the panther sisters are between them and Yerlo.

In the sliver of rainforest that Rumi can see through the opening in the tree's trunk, the first hints of dawn have started to line the edges of leaves, trunks, and vines. "We have only a few minutes until daycoma," he says. "Yerlo, you'll have to fill us in quickly."

"So sleepy," he says, yawning. He shakes his head, gives his own tail a nip. "Wake up, wake up, Yerlo. Okay, here goes. Danger, danger, hold on, Mez, you have to come home and rescue Usha and Derli and Jerlo, I—"

With that the Veil lifts, and Yerlo falls into magical slumber, his snores mixing with Chumba's.

"Feather lice and claw sores!" Sky caws. "Non-shadowwalkers are such a pain."

Mez's lips flick from her teeth and back, over and over. Her tail thrashes, smacking Gogi in the head, Sky on the butt, Gogi on the head, Sky on the butt. "Mez," Gogi says, his words muffled by panther fur, "do you think you could, do you mind—"

"You heard him!" Mez seethes. "Jerlo and Derli and Usha are in trouble. They need rescuing. *Usha* needs rescuing! Can you imagine *that*?"

"Sure, sure," Gogi says. "It sounds serious. In the meantime, do you think you could—?"

Mez's tail thrashes even harder. "I left them on their

own, back when this all started. It's time to go make things right. I have to go back now—to warn them about the lava, too."

"But you won't go without Yerlo and Chumba, of course," Sky says, doing his best to get his tailfeathers out of the way of Mez's tail. "So we have to wait until the Veil lifts. Maybe in the meantime, you could—"

"No, I'm going *now*. Rumi, help me think up some way to transport Yerlo and Chumba."

"I think I could do that," Rumi says from his hiding spot under Gogi's butt. "It would be a sort of litter, with smooth bark on the bottom to cut down on friction. You'd chomp your teeth down on a vine at the front and drag Yerlo and Chumba along. But Mez, while I understand your desire to get home and save the day, it seems to me that, well, in a hierarchy of needs, the fact that this volcano will erupt in three nights and potentially obliterate the entire rainforest—" As Mez bares her teeth, Rumi gets more frantic, waving his suction-cupped fingers in front of him. "—including poor Usha and Jerlo and Derli, wherever they are . . . if we all go off to investigate the panthers, then we'd be losing track of what to do next with the, um, primary task of, um . . . Sky, help me out here."

Before Sky can interject, Mez growls. "But we don't have a plan for what to do about the magma. You said that yourself. And Auriel didn't do anything useful when we were near it."

"We probably weren't in the right spot!" Rumi squeaks, looking at Auriel's blank expression. "And we haven't even discussed what an evacuation might look like!"

"Fine. We'll discuss options, then I'll go save my cousins and aunt," Mez says.

"That's not really how discussions are supposed to work," Rumi grumbles.

Sky caws derisively. "We do have a possible plan. We can join the animals fleeing the volcano, as soon as possible. Maybe the farthest reaches of Caldera will not be destroyed. That is our only option. There is no negotiating with a natural disaster."

"See?" Rumi says defiantly. "We *do* have a plan. Sort of have a plan. Almost have a plan."

"You mean running for our lives?" Mez asks. "Fine. I choose to run for my life in the direction of my homeland."

"I'd like to investigate the 'ocean' we discovered," Sky says. "When lightning strikes and starts a fire, it's rain that puts it out. This magma is like liquid fire. We should evacuate as many animals as we can into the ocean. Maybe we could float on a fallen tree? I say we head toward the giant salty puddle."

"See, even more of a plan," Rumi says. "And does anyone want to go back down there and see if we can wash out the billions of ants that are trying to expose the magma?"

"I nominate Gogi," Lima says.

"I nominate that no one goes down and burns themselves up," Gogi says with uncharacteristic sharpness.

Lima coughs. "Yes, that does seem like a dead end. So to speak."

"I'm going home," Mez says flatly.

"I spent a year with the panthers," Lima says. "If Usha is in trouble, that's a serious thing. And if the source of the problem is this Elemental of Darkness, it really doesn't sound good. Like, at all."

"The panther territory is deep in the interior, unfortunately," Sky says. "Nowhere near the shore."

Mez's low growl intensifies. "I know I'm not being *reasonable* about this, but it's not a *reasonable* thing. My family is in danger. I'm going to help them. Now. Rumi, will you help me figure out how to rig a litter?"

Gogi coughs. "Might I suggest something? We don't all have to be in one place. Perhaps those best suited to each task could go do that one, and we'll reconvene once they're accomplished."

"Good thinking!" Rumi says.

"Thanks, buddy. I thought so too."

"If we do that, I'm going with Mez," Lima says. "I'm an honorary panther, and I'm worried about my new family. She and Chumba and Yerlo are the ones most likely to get into a fight, anyway. They'll need my healing." She looks at Mez. "No offense."

Mez extracts a long claw and smiles. "None taken."

"Rumi and I are the ones most likely to be able to engineer a craft to travel on this ocean we discovered," Sky says. "And I can give Mez my directive to communicate with me from afar, so we can tell her and Lima where exactly to meet us in the escape vessel."

"My water power seems . . . useful for the escape plan," Banu says.

"And I should go with Mez, to help fight," Gogi says.

"Actually, Gogi," Rumi says, "we have no one with offensive magic, and we might need you. I also think we'll need to temper the wood we use to build any craft that can be watertight on the ocean, and repeated exposure to fire and water is probably our best way to accomplish that. If you're willing, I'd like you to stay with us."

Mez nods. "We can spare Gogi."

"Don't take too long to think about it first, or anything," Gogi grumbles.

"Reluctantly," Mez adds. "We can *reluctantly* spare Gogi."

"That's a little better," Gogi sniffs. "And Auriel? What do we do about our mysterious rapidly growing friend?"

They all pause to take in the length of glowing yellow snake. "Hmm," Rumi says.

"He stays with the boys," Mez says, a disdainful look on her face.

"Aww, he's such a pretty accessory, though," Lima says.

"That's final," Mez says.

Lima gives Auriel a squeeze. "I'll miss you!"

Auriel licks the air in response.

"I bet that's how snakes say, 'I'll miss you too,'" Lima says.

Gogi gives her a big hug. "I don't know how I feel about Auriel, but I'll miss *you* tons."

"Well, who wouldn't miss a superhero healing bat?" Lima says bashfully.

Rumi hops out of the monguba hollow. "Now. Let's rig Mez a traveling litter."

Rumi directs Gogi as he uses his agile fingers and toes to tie a liana vine around the edge of a stretch of thick bark, then to use more liana to lash the snoring forms of Chumba and Yerlo to the litter. Mez begins straining against the vine, pulling the contraption forward.

Lima adds her own weight, beating her wings furiously to help, but she's soon exhausted, and rests on Mez's shoulder instead. "Go, Mez, you can do it!" she cheers.

Mez does impressively well, pushing twice her own weight against the straining liana before releasing the vine to address the rest of the companions. "It'll be slow going, but I'll get a head start during the day, and then maybe Yerlo and Chumba can drag *me* for a few hours while I rest after the Veil drops."

Sky turns around and offers his backside in Mez's direction. "You know what to do."

"I'll do the honors," Gogi says. He gets his fingers around one of Sky's crimson feathers, then yanks. Sky caws as the feather comes loose, and Gogi tumbles head over heels. He rigs the feather so it's pinned between the liana vine and the bark of the litter.

"You know how it works by now," Sky tells her. "When you need to communicate with me, hold the directive, and then think of this precise location where it was removed."

"I'll make an echomap," Lima says. "That's the best way."

"Very good. We will use the feather to follow you on your journey, Mez." Sky caws proudly. "My magic has improved so much that all the senses will be involved now, not just vision. I'm working on being able to send you messages through the directive. Stay open to it—you might have me unexpectedly in your mind."

"Lovely," Mez says.

"It *is* lovely!" Rumi protests. "Sharing synapses, how marvelous."

"Well, we're off," Mez says. "I'm sure Chumba and Yerlo would say good-bye if they could."

"Travel safely," Gogi says. The companions take turns giving Mez hugs. Even Sky joins, wrapping his wings awkwardly around Mez for a moment before hurriedly releasing her. Banu gives her a hug, then he sighs and appears to fall asleep, his curved claws wrapped neatly around Mez's ribs.

"Um, Banu, excuse me," Mez says, gently removing the sloth's claws. The moment she's got one up, Banu returns another one to her.

"Oh . . . sorry," he says sleepily as he releases himself to the ground. "You'd make . . . a good branch."

"Great, thanks. Good-bye, everyone!"

"Yep, bye, guys!" Lima adds.

Mez takes up the litter, and with a few ferocious pushes, she and Lima are gone from view.

"Well, gentlemen," Gogi says, hands on his furry hips. "Looks like it's just us boys now."

"To the ocean!" Rumi says. "Wait until you see it in person, Gogi. It's a fascinating place."

"I tend to like drier places more than wetter ones, but I'm willing to suspend judgment until we get there."

Without Chumba, the companions are able to travel on both sides of the Veil. Which is good, since Rumi is reminded all over again that Banu is, um, slow. Rumi knows he would be just as slow—frog legs are made for quick hops to catch prey or avoid death, not for journeying through the rainforest—but of course he can ride on his companions whenever he needs to, which Banu is too big to manage. They tried briefly to see what would happen if Banu rode on Gogi's back. Banu enjoyed it. Gogi, not as much.

During their frequent breaks Gogi experiments with new fire tricks, while Auriel finds the nearest patch of sunlight and soaks it in. In those quieter moments, he seems to grow right in front of Rumi's eyes. When they start a break, Rumi memorizes precisely where Auriel's head is, remembering that it's right alongside the brownish curling piece of grass or what have you, and when they're ready to move on from their rest, it will be two more blades of grass over.

When he's not gauging Auriel's development, Rumi is deep in deliberations with Sky. While he and Sky strategize, Rumi will lie on top of Sky's claws, and it feels like he's finally found a true friend, one who gets and accepts him in all ways.

"So, Rumi," Sky says, "I was scouting out pathways to the ocean, and the most direct one takes us right through a large swamp, devastated a couple of years ago but regrowing. Some of the saplings that emerged from the fallen giants are quite high now."

"How interesting," Rumi says. "We'll go through that swamp. Gogi doesn't mind them as much anymore."

"Yes, well, hrm, this precise swamp . . ."

"Yes?" Rumi asks brightly.

"It's . . . well, it's *your* old swamp, Rumi."

"Oh," Rumi says, gulping. "I see."

"I could find another route," Sky offers, "but anything I picked would make our journey longer."

"No," Rumi says flatly, "we'll go through my old swamp."

"Are you sure?"

"One hundred percent. Moving on. Let's talk about the ark."

It's storming up above, but the canopy siphons away most all of the falling water. Sky leans over a puddle, the surface vibrating and rippling whenever a droplet hits it. He picks up a stick with his beak and drops it onto the surface. "Wood floats, clearly," Sky says. "We all know that. But we don't need a craft just to float. We need it to hold as many land animals as possible."

"That's just about all of us," Rumi says. "I remember what that salty water felt like on my skin when we were near it before. I couldn't swim in the ocean for long."

"Right," Sky says. "So that's why we need to build something that will not only float, but can house animals in dry quarters for what might be a very long time."

"Not just housing. We'll need to pack food for the herbivores . . ." Rumi's voice trails off, as he realizes the implications of what he was about to say next.

"Maybe we institute a no-hunting rule for the carnivores onboard?" Sky says.

Rumi shudders. "But they can't starve, either. Meat eaters make everything so complicated."

"Maybe we could persuade them how good leaves and insects taste," Sky says.

"You try convincing Mez," Rumi says. "I'd like to see how that goes over."

Sky uses his beak to drop two more sticks next to the first. "If we could attach tree trunks together, we could make a raft."

Rumi shakes his head. "Did you see the waves out on the ocean? I think everyone would get knocked off. We need something that could contain us *inside* it."

Sky cocks his head. "I don't understand what you mean."

Grateful for the distraction from the thought of facing his home swamp, and his reduced wind power, Rumi takes some grasses in his fingers and weaves them together with pliable twigs. It makes a crude sphere. "Something like this!"

Sky lets out an admiring caw. "We'd have to weave the grasses tight enough so no water got in."

"I think I could manage that," Gogi says, looking over from where he was braiding fire in the air. Rumi hadn't realized he was listening.

Rumi nods. "You do have agile fingers, Gogi. I'm thinking we could line the inside with marsh grasses, which would provide a water-impermeable layer, and then we'd slather mud inside those. The bits of mud that were on the exterior might stay moist, but then the inside mud layer should dry, so we could rest against it."

Sky's beak clacks excitedly. "We would need to use a variety of woods and grasses. The smaller liana vines will be plentiful, but what kind of wood can withstand so much dousing and drying and more dousing?"

"I . . . might be able to help . . ." Banu says. Rumi startles—he was sure the sloth was asleep. Apparently all his friends are more interested in the deliberations than they let on. "The adult mangrove . . . tree . . . is very bendy. . . . I learned that the hard way . . . when I once . . . chose the wrong place to nap."

"I know just where we'll pass by mangroves," Rumi says darkly.

Sky lays a comforting wing over his friend's back. "We should find them along the waterways that lead to the ocean," he says. "Harder will be the straight pieces we'll use for the main structure. I'm thinking that ironwood would be best, but that won't be near where the mangroves are."

"Ironwood is very heavy," Gogi says, "and we don't have any muscular panther sisters with us now."

"We can . . . use *them*," Banu says. He nods his head in a certain direction. It takes Rumi a few seconds to figure out which direction that is, because, well, sloth nods are quite slow. When he does see what Banu is referring to, though, he hops right into the air.

The daywalker groupies.

"Oh, wow," Gogi says, getting to his feet. "They keep creeping right up on us, don't they?"

The friends work their way through the jungle greenery until they can see better. While they do, Gogi plucks Rumi up from the ground and brings him to his mouth, so he can whisper in the frog's ear. "I saw how you reacted when the mangroves came up."

"You noticed that?" Rumi cheeps in surprise.

"Of course I did. Noticing feelings is my thing. Have out with whatever you have to tell us. It will feel better after, I promise."

Rumi nods. "I'll tell you on the way."

A tapir perks up as the shadowwalkers approach. "Hello there. I hope you don't mind that we eaves-dropped. We didn't want to interrupt."

They're sitting in a polite semicircle, a hodgepodge of animals, three tapirs in the center and an assortment of rats and lizards and songbirds around them. Not the most majestic assortment, but their expressions are full of hope and cheer.

"That's a candle of tapirs," Rumi says. "I've been waiting to have a chance to use that word."

"Hello there," Gogi says. "I am Gogi, Monkey of Fire."

"That's nice," says the tapir.

A songbird chirps at her. "Do you see him?"

"I'm right here," Gogi says, running a hand through his hair.

"Not you. *Him.* The Elemental of Light."

Gogi thumbs in Auriel's direction. "Oh, you mean that guy?"

"It's truly he," the tapir says. "The legends are true!"

Gogi rolls his eyes.

As the glowing snake basks in the sun, the daywalker

pilgrims approach. They sit in a circle around him, watching his every movement, oohing and aahing if Auriel so much as wriggles his tail.

"Hey," Gogi calls over to them. "We'll let you spend time basking in his glow, but on one condition."

"What's that?" the tapir asks. "We'll do anything!"

"Okay. How much can you tapirs carry? And have you ever been to the beach?"

T HE TAPIRS ARE a cheerful lot, nodding and grunt-
ing in acceptance of everything Rumi proposes,
even when it means hefting lumber over bumpy terrain.
Then the group is off. They'll head toward the mangroves, ironwood trees, and finally the beach—passing
through Rumi's home on the way.

Rumi's in his now-customary position on top of Sky's
claws, looking down at the land below as the macaw
scouts. "I want to check in with Mez using your feathers
to link to the one you gave her," Rumi says. "Can I do
that now?"

"Of course," Sky caws back. "Just hold on to one

and send your thoughts to her. Let me know how all the new senses I've been able to work into my magic go. I think you'll find it a more immersive experience than last time."

"I will give you a complete report," Rumi says. "Sky, before I go. I've been thinking. I want to tell Gogi and Banu what you found out in the Cave of Riddles before we get to my home swamp. I need them to understand why I'll be so upset."

"Yes, my friend. I was waiting for you to suggest that. If you're still following Mez through the directive when we're nearing your old home, I'll extract you from the vision."

"Thank you, Sky," Rumi says. "Okay, I'm going in."

Rumi pulls one of Sky's crimson feathers closer to him, careful not to damage the sensitive spot where it enters the macaw's skin. He closes his eyes and thinks of Mez.

Instantly he's there. *Really* there, much more vividly than Sky's magic was ever able to achieve before. There's a slight haze to the scene, but even that could be from volcano smoke instead of any side effect of the magic. Rumi watches through the directive while Yerlo draws the panther sisters up short. "This is where I last saw them," he says.

The panthers go still, sniffing around the broken fronds of a fern that must have once housed a den. From her position hanging upside down from Mez's neck, Lima wriggles her nose. "I don't smell any panthers."

"I do," Chumba says. "This way."

Yerlo gives an impressed yowl as he follows. "Chumba's tracking skills have always been the best in the family," Mez says as they slink off, slow and silent through the undergrowth.

Picking up on the sisters' unease, even Lima goes quiet, riding the air currents so her wing beats can't reveal their location.

Chumba brings them up a tree, claws digging deep into wet and mossy wood. It's a giant fig, so tall that its branches are as large as normal-sized trees, interlocking to form what feels like a copy of the jungle floor. There are fish in pools up there, tadpoles waiting to turn into frogs, all a good hundred panther-lengths over the ground.

"Aunt Usha?" Chumba whispers.

Panthers don't generally make dens in the trees, but here is Usha's voice, and the voice of a young panther, coming from a leafy corner of the canopy. "Chumba? Is that you?"

A breeze crops up, swaying the tree. Chumba, Mez, and Yerlo lower their ears in deference, casting their chins toward the branches. Even Lima joins them, bowing her little bat head, ears flopping and fluttering in the night breeze.

There's a shift in the blacks of night, and what Rumi had thought was a starless patch of sky reveals it to be a panther slinking along a branch. When it turns, green eyes glitter.

"Usha," Mez breathes. Rumi watches from the vantage point of the feather strapped to her as she slinks forward, sniffing Usha's tail. Up closer, he can see what has bothered Mez. The regal panther, though still large and strong, has patches of missing fur, revealing deep scars along her body. One ear is ragged and torn. Her fur sticks out at rough angles, unlike the sleek lines of a healthy panther.

Rumi knows how much intimidation is mixed into the panthers' love for their aunt, how she was a model of strength for them. To see her this way must be awful.

Another panther noses along after Usha. Like Yerlo, this one has lost the puffball look of the youngest panthers, but still makes her way along awkwardly, on oversized paws. She has a scar running over her nose, splitting it nearly in two. "Jerlo," Chumba cries, nuzzling her cousin. "What happened to you?"

"The Elemental of Darkness," Jerlo says miserably. "The Elemental of Darkness happened to us."

Usha winces as she lowers her body to the branch. "You will need to face the enemy, so I should tell you what happened. Maybe you can learn from us, and have a chance to stop him. I don't think it's likely that any of us will succeed, but you have to try."

Usha places most of her attention on Chumba. Rumi knows from Mez that though the panther sister is missing a front paw, she has proven a scrappy and resourceful fighter, and is next in line to lead the panther family.

"We have heard some from Yerlo," Mez says. "He says that there is a being some animals call the Elemental of Darkness. It sent minions after us."

Usha chuckles darkly. "It's true. I will never call him the Elemental of anything, but he is happy to call himself that. I will bring you to see the Elemental of Darkness so you can see the truth for yourselves. You're our only hope that his foul goals will not be achieved."

"Foul goals?" Lima squeaks.

"Follow me," Usha says darkly. "It's simpler for you to see what I'm talking about for yourselves."

Despite the evident pain in her limbs, Usha makes her way along the branch and slinks to one lower, then another. Jerlo follows after, quickly joined by Yerlo and the panther sisters, Lima back to riding tucked under Mez's chin.

"After we cross the marshy stream up ahead, we keep absolute silence," Usha intones. "No one must hear us."

Mez is almost ready to cross the stream, but stops short. She looks back at Yerlo, Jerlo, Usha. Yerlo, Jerlo, Usha. She sucks in her breath. "Aunt Usha . . . where's Derli?"

Jerlo and Yerlo close their eyes and look away, tails sinking. Usha's eyes narrow, and her scarred ribs quiver with her rapid breathing. "I cannot say the words," she says, her voice husky with emotion. "Besides, the words will not change what's happened. You will see the truth for yourselves soon enough. Now, *silence*."

Usha has stepped across the marshy stream. Rumi follows along as the panthers drop into hunting posture, tails low and ears back, eyes alert to any sign of prey or danger. The reek of pantherfear wafts up through the thick jungle air.

Lima alights on Mez's back, right in front of the feather. Rumi gets a very close-up view of her backside. Bats don't really have butts to speak of, he realizes. As if she's aware that Rumi's there watching through the feather, Lima turns around and gives it a tender pat. She's saying hello, across the vast distance between them. Lima gives him a wink and a wing thumbs-up. The gesture brings tears to Rumi's eyes.

For a while the panthers pass through the jungle in perfect silence. Then Mez hisses, and Lima's attention whips forward.

"I don't understand. How can this be?" Mez whispers.

Unfortunately, Lima's backside is covering Rumi's view. He can't tell what Mez is talking about until she jumps to the next tree over—which is when he can see, in a straight line along the ground, perfectly spaced hirsuta trees. Their exact alignment goes against every rule of the chaotic jumble of the rainforest.

Far more ominous, though, is the fact that the trees are on *fire*. The flames are small licks, just enough to cast a ruddy glow in the moist night air, but it adds even more ominous layers to the scene. While they watch, unnerved, giant moths and click beetles buzz into the fires, flaring out and falling smoldering to the ground.

"The blazes are perfectly controlled," Chumba says, her surprise making her forget Usha's orders not to speak. "Who's making that happen?"

"Someone with a magical ability to control fire," Mez spits.

"But that's silly," Lima whispers. "Gogi is the only one we know who can do that, and he wouldn't make this creepy scene. Also, he's not even *here*." Having worked herself up into a righteous fit, she slaps a nearby trunk. "Ouch. That's definitely real fire. Just so you ladies know."

Yerlo raises his sensitive nose. "Do you scent that?"

Usha nods. "He's not too near, but in the area. Be silent, everyone."

They follow as she slinks around the edge of the hirsutas. The trees unnerve Rumi, even far away, because of the firelight upon them. But their orderliness doesn't bother him as much as it seems to bother his friends. They break the chaotic nature of the rainforest for a perfectly natural reason: hirsuta trees are the homes of lemon ants—the two species have a relationship, where the ants get to use the tree as their home, and in return they kill off any competing plants and ants. That's why the clearing is so sparse, why there are no other trees blocking their view, why the firelight is able to cast such eerie shadows on the open space. But his friends probably don't know such things. Their surreal surroundings must be extra terrifying to them.

The panthers and Lima pass along a valley of carnivorous pitcher plants, their funnel-shaped openings built to channel in scores of insects. Some of them reach higher than the panthers themselves. Low-hanging branches knit the sky above, so that the air becomes even more close, even more still. Any sound that the panthers made would carry easily through the nearby forest, over even the droning of the grasshoppers, cicadas, and crickets.

"Pew," Lima says all of a sudden, waving a wing in front of her nose. "Does anyone else smell that?"

Usha goes perfectly still, foreleg frozen in midair. The other panthers mirror her. For a moment Rumi worries that the directive is broken, because it looks just like time has stopped.

Lima is the first to eventually move, hopping to the top of Mez's head, probably to get a better view. She puts her wings over her mouth.

Rumi sees why soon enough. There's a nightwalker cult.

That's the only way Rumi can think of to describe it. The rainforest opens out into a murky clearing, with a low pond crisscrossed by drier patches of grassy soil. The whole area is full of animals. Unlike how they would usually behave, these nightwalkers are out in the open, in a semicircle. There are frogs and toads, an ocelot, owls and bats, Goliath birdeater tarantulas, a couple of boa constrictors, and who knows what other nightwalkers hidden in the dark. What—or who—they're circling around, Rumi can't yet see.

The nightwalker cultists sway in the firelight, smoke hazing the air around them. None of them seems to have noticed the approaching panthers—Usha's instinct to go stock-still was a good one. For now, at least, they can observe the cult in peace.

Each of the nightwalkers that's large enough is wearing a flower somewhere on its body—between the ears for the ocelot, behind the head for the snakes. Not just any flower; these are thick, drooping, and waxy, mottled in red and white. Worst of all, even through the directive Rumi can detect a pungent, rotting odor. Carrion blossoms. They smell like rotting flesh to attract pollinating insects. This cult seems to have some other use for them, though. Rumi assumes it's a mark of membership.

Rumi follows along as Mez eases into motion, eking her way through the bushes, getting nearer to the cult. She's nearly noiseless, passing forward on soft paws, Chumba equally quiet beside her. Even Lima is somehow managing to stay silent, keeping her wings tight around her mouth as she rides on her perch.

The stench of the carrion flowers grows stronger, and Rumi starts to hear chanting. The nightwalkers are saying one syllable over and over. Their voices are so soft and reverential that Rumi can't make out what they're saying.

Mez slinks even closer—just a few lengths away from the nearest nightwalker, a boa constrictor—and reaches out a paw to fold down a fern leaf. Rumi can sense her body go rigid when she sees what's on the other side.

The Elemental of Darkness is in the center of the circle.

The Elemental of Darkness is Mist.

A good half a size bigger than he was before, he sits tall on his haunches, surveying the surrounding animals with a magisterial air. Though he still has the dramatic facial scar that came after animals hunting for Mez mistakenly attacked him, Mist otherwise looks in good health. His white fur is soft and sleek and full of volume, and for the first time since Rumi has ever seen him, his brows are smooth and his lips unsnarling. He's . . . calm.

Mist's stature's not just from his increased size, though. Rumi focuses in on what's below him.

Mist is standing on what Rumi at first assumes to be a hill of fresh soil, but then he sees it's something much worse. At the base of the hill emerges a hoof here, an arm there—it's a daywalker burial mound. How many slain animals have been hastily dumped within, Rumi doesn't know—but it's a lot.

Mist swivels to take in the assembled nightwalkers, soaking in their adulation. As he shifts, Rumi can see that beside Mist is a young panther, the same size as Yerlo and Jerlo. His paws have been bound with one length of liana, so that all four are wrenched together.

He lies on his side, eyes scrunched shut. He might be unconscious. Rumi can see from the movement of his scrawny rib cage that his breaths are shallow and rapid.

"Oh no," Chumba whispers through gritted teeth. "Poor Derli."

"Mist showed up at our den two moon cycles ago," Usha hisses. "We had heard about the demise of the Ant Queen, of course, and your hand in it, but we did not yet know that Mist had worked to help the Ant Queen in return for her favors. That information he scornfully told us only after his plan was in motion."

"His plan?" Mez asks.

"He challenged Usha for control!" Jerlo says, hissing.

"He what?" Mez asks, tail thrashing. The scent of pantherfear rises from her.

"Mez," Chumba warns. "Don't let them detect us."

"What does that even *mean*, challenging Usha for control?" Lima whispers.

Usha's whiskers prick. "He broke no rules by challenging me. It's long been panther ritual that any member of a family may challenge for control, and the results of the one-on-one combat are binding. I knew that one of your generation might challenge me someday, but I did not expect it to come for many drops of the Veil yet. I was unprepared."

"It wasn't a fair fight," Jerlo says, shaking her head. "Mist hadn't told Usha about the magic he got when you destroyed the Ant Queen."

"He did not have to. I accepted his challenge, and then I lost the fight. That makes the handover of power legitimate." As is her usual way, Usha shows little emotion, instead keeping up her regal air. But even across a long distance, Rumi can see how the luster has dulled in her eyes, the defeat that droops her whiskers despite her defiant posture.

"The last we saw Mist, he ran into the swirling magical energies the Ant Queen left behind," Mez says. "He disappeared after that."

"As you can see, he's far larger and stronger than me now," Usha says. "Even if he had stayed his normal size, he is still in his youthful prime. My muscles are not as strong as they once were. He might have won without needing any magic at all."

Mez gapes at her dispirited aunt.

"Don't speak like that, Mother," Jerlo interjects. "You could have beaten him. Mist got lucky."

"I wish I had beaten him," Usha says. "I would have fought to the death if I'd known he was planning all this."

"What *is* this? What's he doing?" Chumba says.

"He's done something no other panther has done," Yerlo says. "He's exercised the right of dominion across species lines."

"Right of dominion? What's that? Can I have one?" Lima asks.

"Panthers are the apex of the rainforest power structure," Mez whispers. "Normally that's left unstated, since we have no use for any additional power beyond being able to eat whomever we choose."

"Yeah, it's hard to imagine wanting much more than that," Lima says, nodding.

"All the same, we panthers talk a lot about our right of dominion," Chumba adds.

Mez nods ruefully. "It's one of my least favorite things about panthers. We believe we are totally separate from the other animals, and because of that we have the power to do what we please with the rest."

"Is anything worse than eating the other animals?" Lima asks.

"A very good question," Usha says darkly. "My answer would have been no . . . until I saw what Mist has done. Hush. He's about to speak."

"Gather close, my allies," Mist says. "I have an announcement."

The panthers nestle themselves more thoroughly into the greenery while Mist takes in the assembled nightwalkers. Smoky firelight fills the humid air, as the nightwalkers sway and watch, their carrion flower decorations dotting the clearing.

The nightwalkers press closer to Mist. Among them are predators and prey, and a few of them startle at the unexpected closeness to sworn enemies. They begin to chatter, but Mist stares them each in the eye in turn, then lifts out a paw, pads up. He lets out a burst of fire. *It's confirmed*, Rumi thinks. *Mist has powers over fire.*

Awed, the nightwalker cultists go silent.

"You remember how we all lost our powers momentarily while the lens was redistributing the magical energy of the eclipse?" Mez whispers. "I'm starting to have some suspicions about the source of Mist's power."

Chumba, Usha, Jerlo, and Yerlo nod somberly. Lima nods. Then stops. She looks between them. "Wait. What is it?"

"That *is* Gogi's power," Mez whispers. "Or at least a sliver of it."

"Yikes," Lima says. "I wonder who else's powers he got."

As if in response, Mist opens his mouth and sends out a whirlwind of air that catches the flames, sending them in a swirling tornado that rises into the night sky before dissipating in a rain of sparks.

It's not as big an effect as Rumi would have been able

to achieve back when his magic was at full power, but it seems Mist also has *some* power over the wind. *Rumi's* power. Did he take it, does that explain Rumi's reduced abilities? But then again, none of the other shadowwalkers have had their magic reduced in the same way. There must be some other reason for Rumi's wind cramp.

Fire is especially impressive to nightwalkers, whose eyes are adapted to create images from even the smallest amount of light. They are literally dazzled by Mist, eyes blinking rapidly and streaming tears. Through the transmitted vision of the feather, Rumi isn't hit as strongly by the image, and so he can watch without pain as Mist, after staring about the crowd to gauge the impression he's making, disappears from view.

Invisibility. Mez's power. He's got that one, too.

Each of them who was at the titanic fight against the Ant Queen during the lunar eclipse, when the magic of Caldera was released and reshuffled—Mist has absorbed some of their powers. This had been Auriel's plan originally, until he died and was resurrected. Mist has accomplished what Auriel was never able to do.

The nightwalker cultists recover, losing their dazed looks as they scan about the clearing, eyes streaming tears as they search for their leader. As they do, Rumi feels his blood begin to race. Panthers are very good at hiding, but the combined searching of all these nightwalkers will soon uncover them.

Thankfully, Mist doesn't take too long to deliver his reentrance. Jets of flame lance into the night sky, and then Mist appears in the midst of the group of nightwalker cultists, still balanced on the burial mound as he shoots flames from his tail and the backs of his paws. The assembled nightwalkers shout and screech and bray in horror.

"My allies," Mist says, "I hope that display has impressed on you the horror of fire. The volcano is only starting to become active—what you have yet witnessed of fire is but a mere flicker compared to what will happen in a few nights when the volcano goes off. We must begin our nightly hunt for daywalkers. It is they who have generated the black clouds at the horizon, it is they who have caused the rumbling of the earth, it is they who are the source of all Caldera's evils. They must be punished!"

"Mist, what are you doing?" Mez hisses softly.

Rumi knows that of course Mist's claims don't make any sense, that there's no daywalker conspiracy to set the volcano off. But the claims energize his followers, set them into hooting and hissing. Whether Mist believes what he's saying or not, his words are working.

"I have proved my commitment to our shared goal," Mist says. "You witnessed as I defeated my own mother in ritual combat. She is in her prime, and I should not have been able to best her, but I did. I should not have ever wanted to contest her, but I did for your sakes. Look what else I have sacrificed: here before you is my brother, punished and imprisoned, at our collective mercy because he dared to resist me. You need no more evidence of my devotion. That is why, when I ask you to do what I am about to ask of you, you must act and not question my words. I deserve at least that from you in return for everything I have given up."

Rumi sees a mixture of horror and morbid curiosity in Mez's and Chumba's expressions. Lima flicks her floppy round ears, a sure sign she's not sure what's going on. Usha's eyes are downcast. She's clearly overcome.

Rumi's mind races. Mist has taken all of their powers, from Gogi to Rumi to Mez to . . . Sky. Divination. That's almost the most fearsome. What does Mist *know*?

"We are about to face our greatest battle, my minions," Mist says. "The night I foretold has arrived. There are adversaries in our midst."

Mez's and Chumba's ears flatten, and they shrink deeper into the shadows of the fern. Lima chirps in fear. But even if they know what's coming next, they can't make a break for it, not if doing so would reveal their location.

Mist's gaze trains more and more toward the fern

where the companions are hiding. "We all know how idiotic daywalkers are," he says. "They could never come up with a plot to destroy our land all on their own. They need the help of the shadowwalkers, the evil beings that ushered in this time of troubles. The evil beings that maimed *me*, your Elemental of Darkness. And those shadowwalkers have heard about our movement to cleanse the forest of daywalkers. They have come with the arrogance to think they can stop us."

Murmurs and hisses. "Just tell us where they are!" calls one of the boa constrictors.

"Once we destroy this threat, you and your Elemental of Darkness will be free to save the land from the black clouds, from the coming lava, to put an end to this time of troubles."

"Sweet guano, this is bad," Lima chirps.

Mez and Chumba shrink deeper into the ferns.

"Where are these enemies?" an owl hoots.

"When I count down from three, the battle begins," Mist says, his eyes on a fern—the very fern where the panthers are hiding. The cats crouch as low as they can into their camouflage.

"Three," Mist says.

Chumba's claws extend, while Lima silently flits to a higher branch.

"Two," Mist says.

Usha begins to growl, hackles rising.

Mez slinks forward to be the first into the fight, going invisible as she creeps to the exposed edge of the fern.

"One," Mist says.

The clearing goes still, all attention on Mist.

He draws back the remnants of his lips, exposing long teeth. Rumi waits for him to speak, but that's not what Mist does next.

He sends a fireball out of his mouth, right to the fern hiding Mez, Chumba, Usha, Jerlo, Yerlo, and Lima.

As the fireball streams toward the directive, the red filling more and more of the view, Rumi is suddenly yanked out of the vision. All is crisping flame, Sky's magic strong enough to project the actual heat to him, hot enough to make his skin sizzle and stretch . . . and then the air is cool and moist, his vision full of soft brown—the backside of a tapir.

"Hey, hey!" Sky's concerned voice says. "Rumi! Stop screaming. You're blowing my feathers all around."

Of course Rumi hadn't realized that he *was* screaming. He closes his mouth. His throat is aching. "Mez and Chumba and Lima," he sputters. "They're in trouble."

"Is it anything that we can fix right now?" Sky asks patiently.

"No," Rumi gasps.

"Then take a moment before you go back in," Sky says. "Your pulse is racing, and you're almost hyperventilating."

"You don't understand, you don't understand—"

"Shh. Rumi, you're out of control. Your heart."

"Okay, okay. I'm calming down. Now send me back in."

"No, you're not. You're still trembling all over. You won't be any help to anyone if you let this do you in. I'm still receiving the directive's vision," Sky says. "It's storing in my feathers themselves. You can go right back to the panthers as soon as you've calmed down, and it will be like no time has passed. I'll basically put you back in time. You won't miss a thing, okay? But I don't want your heart to stop in the meantime."

"But—"

"This isn't a choice, Rumi."

"Sky. My wind," Rumi says. "Was I . . . ?"

"You didn't release much wind. Just enough to muss my feathers."

"I'm relieved, actually," Rumi says as the thudding in his veins begins to subside. "I didn't want to hurt anyone accidentally."

"I bet you were worried about that," Sky says. "It's understandable, given what we both know. About that, Rumi. I woke you up because we're nearing—well, you'll see for yourself. Just on the other side of that stand of ironwood trees, there's your old swamp."

Rumi gauges the speed of the lumbering tapir beneath him. "So I have only a few minutes?"

"Just about," Sky says. "Should I call Gogi over? It will be easier to tell him ahead of time."

"I know, I know," Rumi says. "Let me do it. Gogi!" he trills.

A flash, then his monkey friend is beside them. "Hey, you're back with us," he says. "How's Mez?"

"Not good," Rumi says. "Mist has a cult worshipping him, and he used the rule of dominion to take control of the nearby jungle. He usurped Usha, and now he just discovered that the panthers and Lima are there, and he's cast a fireball, one of *your* fireballs, Gogi, and it's heading right for them."

"Rumi, don't forget to breathe," Sky warns. "We can all check in with them after, through my feather memory. You're not ready to go back in yet."

"Yes," Rumi says, willing his breathing to go regular and even. "We'll go back to the panthers as soon as we can."

"Wait, we're not finding out right away whether they're okay?" Gogi says. "Something is more urgent than that?"

"I've got too much going on in my brain to make it safe," Rumi says with a sad croak.

"Whoa, buddy, I can tell this is major," Gogi says. "Okay. I'm listening."

"Sky, your directive power," Rumi says. "Could you transmit our memory of the vision itself, what we saw with the guardians in the Cave of Riddles?"

Sky cocks his head. "I suppose I could try. I wasn't consciously embedding the memory into a feather at the time, unlike what I'm doing with Mez's directive right now, so some of the details might be shaded by my imperfect recollection. But let's see what I can turn up."

"Who's doing what to who now?" Gogi asks.

Sky peers at Rumi. "Are you going to be okay?"

Rumi nods sadly, throat pouch quivering. "This memory is depressing instead of worrying. Quite a different emotional effect."

"Here goes," Sky says. "Just grab onto a feather. I'll pull you back out once the recollection is over."

As one, monkey and frog reach out and touch Sky.

*An egg in a clutch, glued to the underside of a leaf, eyes behind clear membranes, watching the sun above, then the moon above, then the sun. Some neighbors are taken, some remain. A wasp hauls eggs away, one by one, until Rumi's father comes by to scare it off.*

*It's not easy being an egg.*

*Rumi is one of the last to emerge, kicking his tail fin, gills pumping furiously as he works his way past the gooey remains of his siblings' eggs. A baffling few minutes, then his father is near. Rumi wriggles onto his backside, gluing himself to skin. Lurching into motion, Rumi's father carries whatever offspring he can find up the side of a tree, higher and higher into the canopy, leaving them in a water-filled leaf high over the forest floor before going back down to ferry another batch.*

*Rumi and his siblings eat and wriggle and grow, chowing down on algae as soon as it appears. That and the occasional mosquito larvae—yum. Though he can't talk yet, Rumi gets to know some of the personalities of his tadpole siblings. There's Shy Rumi and Ferocious Rumi and Thoughtful Rumi and more. They grow and grow, and soon the leaf can barely hold them all. It bows and bends with each rain droplet.*

*His hind limb buds can't come soon enough. Eventually they're there, and Rumi can swim-walk, leveraging the beginnings of his legs to get around. His body tail reabsorbs, his front legs burst through his chest, his gills start to feel gummy as they close up. Ouch. But at least soon he'll be able to take his first gasp of air!*

*Whew. Air in his lungs. It feels amazing.*

*His father's there, and Rumi clambers onto his back. His mother is near too, and other froglets climb onto her.*

*Rumi gets a good look at his home swamp for the first time. Dank and misty, giant trees shading the starlight, mud and tasty ants everywhere.*

*It's simply perfect.*

*He gives up on his gills, and opens his mouth to take in some more of that amazing air.*

*It goes in. When it goes out, though . . . !*

*Rumi goes zooming through the air, landing on his back many frog-lengths away from his family. He lies there, stunned. What just happened to him?*

*Rumi hops back over, making sure to breathe as shallowly as he can, so he doesn't go flying again. But just a short while later, he gets distracted by his first tangy fire ant snack. He exclaims in glee, and the force of the air leaving his mouth sends him hurtling.*

*His siblings watch with wide froggy eyes as he hops his way back.*

*He shrugs when they ask what happened, keeps his gaze trained on the leaves around him. Nothing to see here, just trying to fit in.*

*Later, when the Veil rises and Rumi's siblings are all finding hiding places to wait out their daycoma, Rumi finds himself wide awake. Strange. So much strangeness. No tree* frog is meant to be up during the day! The sun is harsh on young amphibian skin, so he has nothing more to do with his day than wander around the shady underside of a fern where he and his siblings are resting, back and forth and back and forth, as the rays change in angle. He experiments with letting out slight gusts, watching the tips of the ferns sway. He sends out bigger gusts, watching the branches of the next tree over sway. Hmm!

He stops experimenting for a while, but then the questions scratching his mind grow too great: why wind? Where does this power come from? Why do none of the other frogs have it? Can he direct it to a tiny spot? Can he make it blow all over? Can he use it to fly? Rumi takes in his breath and holds it while he counts to ten, savoring the buzz of magical energy fighting to escape his lungs.

What if he blew the hardest gust he could, to learn the limits of his power?

He can at least see if he can make the highest branches of that fig sway, the one just barely in view. That shouldn't be too risky an experiment.

Rumi creeps forward, so that he's outside the hiding spot his parents chose for their young frogs, at the edge of a sunbeam on the rainforest floor.

He takes in the largest breath that he can.

He sets his gaze on the treetop in the distance.

He aims.

*He prepares to release.*

*That's when he's attacked.*

*Rumi hadn't even noticed the motionless snake, perfectly camouflaged around the nearby tree branch, until it strikes. Fangs slash through the blinding sunlight, heading right for his tender belly.*

*There's no time to run, no time to dodge. There's only one thing to do, which is to open his mouth and release all the air he was holding in.*

*The fangs disappear as the snake is blasted across the clearing, pulverized against a tree trunk.*

*Rumi has no idea what happens next, only that he too is flying through the air, that trees are cracking, that insects and birds and mammals and other frogs are soaring, maybe his parents and siblings, there's debris everywhere, swirling through the sky and clouding the sun. A sound like thunder is coming from his own mouth as he flies, then he hits something in the grayness where there used to be sunlight, and all is still.*

*When he comes to, Rumi sees that he's somewhere else entirely. A ruined land of fallen trees, where soil has been uprooted and flung everywhere, where the land itself has scattered, dirtying everything. A landscape whose normal sounds are gone, replaced by the moans of dying animals.*

*He staggers to his feet.*

*Father? Mother?*

*Where are his siblings?*

*What's happened to his forest?*

*His head and body aching, Rumi wanders through the swampy land, hopping this way and that, calling out for the other Rumis of his birth group. There is no answer. No birds call, no insects chirp. All's quiet and eerie, the only sound the drip of rainwater on ravaged earth. He struggles to get his thoughts in order, to remember what might have happened.*

*A horrible thought grows in Rumi's mind, one that he can't entirely face. If he lets it wriggle its way to the front, it will undo him entirely.*

*No. It's not possible that he did this.*

*Finally he sees another living creature. It's a big frog, a cane toad, a terrible wound on its back already beginning to scab over as it staggers through the growth. Only a creature as massive and fat as this one could have survived the typhoon that devastated this rainforest.*

*Frogs are the worst predators of other frogs. Though Rumi hopes for answers, he knows this one is more likely to eat him than to answer questions. He eases forward delicately, not announcing himself early.*

*The cane toad, though, is a hunter perfectly attuned to its surroundings. Its focus lands right on Rumi, where he thinks he's safely hiding in the shadows of an uprooted tree. "Everything in this part of the rainforest is dead. All my family is dead. Only I was sturdy enough to survive. How did you survive this disaster, little frog, so little that you still have fresh gill marks on your throat?"*

*Rumi doesn't answer. Maybe there's hope this predator doesn't know precisely where he is. Besides, Rumi doesn't* have *an answer.*

*"Then Big Rumi will tell you," the giant cane toad says. "I woke from daycoma to find our rainforest demolished. Just a short ways over there, though, the rainforest is completely intact. This was no storm. There was no flooding. This disaster reeks of magic."*

*Rumi hangs his little head. The cane toad's words ring true. It was magic. It was Rumi's magic that created the whirlwind that destroyed all these lives. Finally he speaks. "I have to confess. It's my fault. I did this. If you want to eat me, I won't stop you. I deserve it."*

*Big Rumi pauses, then takes a shuddering step forward, his jowls rippling. "I did not expect you to give yourself up so easily. You cannot blame me for taking my revenge, little one."*

*Rumi looks up sadly, feeling his toxins beginning to coat his skin. "I'm poisonous. If you kill me, you will die as well."*

*Big Rumi nods. "Then that will be my destiny. I will die in order to punish you. It will be worth it."*

*Rumi chirps quietly, undone by the enormity of the devastation he's wrought. He would gladly accept Big Rumi's punishment. But then another animal would die, the only other one to survive Rumi's magical cyclone. His wrongdoing would be absolute.*

*He won't let another creature's death be on his hands, even if it's a murderous bully like Big Rumi.*

*And so Rumi turns and flees the swamp, Big Rumi right on his heels.*

9

THE VISION ENDS, and Rumi is looking at his friends' concerned expressions. Sky, who already saw this vision long before in the Cave of Riddles, stares closely at Rumi's face, probably to see how he's dealing with the trauma. Gogi shakes his head and whistles. "Wow. Heavy stuff."

Rumi kneads his suction-cupped fingers against one another. "I should probably keep going, and get this over with."

"Wait, there's more?" Gogi asks.

"Well, this all came out because of the challenges of the Cave of Riddles," Rumi says. "It all plays into how that ended up. And maybe into why my wind powers are reduced?"

Gogi nods. "Then go ahead, friend. We want to hear everything."

*I woke from my dream into the complete darkness. I didn't know where I was, or why I was there. All that was going through my mind was what happened to my home. Family, friends—and enemies as well—all killed because of my magical power. Because of who I was.*

*Even though I was deep in the Cave of Riddles, it felt like Big Rumi was there too, that he was still chasing me down. I was frantic. I hopped without direction, bouncing against walls and floor, bashing my head against stone outcroppings, Sky squawking nearby as he tried to find me in the darkness to calm me down.*

*Then the soft velvety creatures were back, touching my face, communicating with me. "You have revealed your true heart to us, Rumi Mosquitoswallow. Your intellect is mighty, but your heart thirsts for answers to what* might *be at times when it should instead find rest and acceptance with what* is. *You would seek to find the limits of knowledge about what the lens might do, when you ought to be thinking about what it ought to do."*

*"What does that mean?" I croaked, though I had come*

to suspect that the foreign creatures knew my thoughts without my needing to speak them.

"It means that we have decided that you are unworthy of the lens."

"Unworthy?" I said back, my voice narrowing to a mere chirp. "How can this be? We need the lens to save Caldera!"

"We guardians are not here to measure your purpose, only to measure your worth. This decision is final."

I hurled myself to the ground. Of course I was unworthy. My guilt had always told me that, and now it was going to cost Caldera its future. "I'm sorry," I wailed, "I'm so sorry."

"Hush, small frog," the voice said. "You were the only one found unworthy."

I raised my head. "What do you mean?"

"I accept," Sky cawed. "I will care for the lens."

"Wait," I said. "Sky is the one you choose?"

Sky squawked indignantly.

"While we were in your mind, little Rumi, we were also in Sky's," the guardians said. "He was rescued from neglect by Auriel. He expressed great loyalty to the snake who saved him, and it was that very loyalty to which you and your friends took exception. We consider him to be a cautious steward, unlikely to have his mind swayed in the moment to moment. He has a seriousness of purpose that makes him a suitable guardian. We have made our selection."

"Thank you for this honor," Sky said. "I will do my best."

There was another grinding sound, and then a crack of light appeared in the chamber's roof. In the sudden light, I could see ribbonlike shapes moving around us. These were the velvety tentacles that we'd felt, but I still couldn't tell what sort of animal they were.

I wanted to investigate further, but my attention was drawn to the crack of light. It widened until it became a blinding opening in the ground, waves of light shining about the chamber, like stray rays of sunshine finding their way into a nightwalker den. From the chasm rose a circular object that had hardened clear stone in its center. It sent the light from below skittering around, concentrating and refracting it.

The lens.

The marvelous object was held up by the ribbon creatures, bobbing on the backs of their leechlike forms. "Take it," the guardian's voice said.

Sky clattered forward on the stone floor and then hopped into the air, working his claws around the lens.

The guardian's voice came back, unexpectedly loud. "Our task is done! The Cave of Riddles is no more! We will help you escape, but you must act quickly!"

Suddenly there was more light in the room, enough to illuminate the whole chamber. With a shivering and grinding sound, the ceiling began to fragment and fall apart, the sandstone shivering into tiny particles that rained down on us. "On my back, Rumi!" Sky called.

He didn't need to ask twice. I gathered all the strength in my back legs and hopped, landing in the midst of his feathers. I got my grip around them. "I'm ready!" I called.

Sky took to the air, managing the weight of the lens and dodging the worst swirls of sandstone as he stroked toward the daytime sky, his wing beats sending up powerful gusts of new sand.

Everything in me told me to scrunch my eyes shut and wait until it was over, but somehow I managed to keep my eyes open enough to look below. My thirst for knowledge wouldn't let me shrink away this time. That's why I was able to see that the velvety tentacles weren't animals at all but plants, broad leaves of witch's tongue that some magic had brought to move and speak. We'd been communicating with something that wasn't at all of the animal world! Now it would be sealed away, under the fallen cliff. What a missed opportunity for information.

True to their word, the guardians were careful that the crumbling cave didn't send any huge chunks of stone down on us—of course they didn't want to bury the first guardians to come through and rescue the lens. It was horribly noisy, but Sky managed to fly me and the lens from there.

As soon as we were up and out, I looked back down. The tumbling ancient earth of the cliffs revealed broad sections of exposed rock, with bones embedded in them. All sorts of animals, some of them much bigger than any animals we know of in Caldera today. But there was no time to investigate—it was back to you, to the rest of the shadowwalkers.

We took only a moment's rest on the beach at the edge of Caldera, then we started back toward the ruined ziggurat, where we had planned on meeting you. And we did, just in the nick of time, allowing us to destroy the Ant Queen. But you know that part.

NCE RUMI'S FINISHED, there's a long silence as
Gogi processes his story.

"Ever since then, my magic has been reduced,"
Rumi says morosely.

Banu, who finally made it over just as the vision was
ending, scratches his backside as he looks between the
flabbergasted shadowwalkers. "What did I miss?"

Gogi pats Banu's head numbly. "I'll catch you up
later."

Gogi's been riveted, barely blinking even though
his eyes are bloodshot with fatigue. Sky, despite having
lived through it all with Rumi, is equally rapt. Auriel
held still the whole time, tongue tasting the air as he

listened. Or maybe didn't listen. Rumi's still not sure what he's capable of.

His tale over, Rumi wrings his hands. "So that's all of it," he says, directing his voice into the mud. "My curiosity killed hundreds of creatures. The guardians refused to give me the lens because I was . . . unworthy." Tears, long held back, water his eyes. "And now even my magic is nearly gone. Because I'm evil."

"Wow," Banu says. "I really missed a lot, huh?"

Rumi covers his face with his hands. Why isn't Gogi saying anything?

He cracks his eyes open to see that Gogi's attention, surprisingly enough, is on Sky. "We wouldn't have defeated the Ant Queen if you hadn't been judged worthy of the lens. We've been hard on you, but you have redeemed yourself many times over. Thank you, Sky."

Sky inclines his head awkwardly. "I did collaborate with the snake who betrayed us all. Your resistance to me was understandable."

Auriel startles and gazes deeply at Sky.

Gogi then does something Rumi never would have expected: he grooms Sky. He clearly doesn't know what to do with all the feathers, slinking his fingers through and patting them, wiping the oil off on his thighs. Nevertheless, grooming is a very meaningful gesture coming from a social animal like Gogi. "So, Rumi," Gogi says, his eyes glittering. "About your home swamp."

Rumi's eyes go wet again, and he can't stop his body from trembling. "I'm so sorry!"

"It wasn't your fault, you big silly," Gogi finishes. "It was clearly all a misunderstanding. I don't know why you've been letting it bother you so much."

"But . . . but I destroyed them all," Rumi whimpers.

"Oh gosh. Rumi, get over here," Gogi says. He opens up his arms.

Rumi shakes his head, miserable.

Gogi pads over from Sky and carefully wraps his tail around Rumi. Then he curls the rest of his body around him. "Rumi, I know I'm speaking for Mez and Chumba and Lima when I say we love you. No one should hold a mistake against you. I just feel bad that you kept this all inside for so long. You should have told us right away."

"But I, but I . . ." Rumi sputters.

"You are forgiven, you dope," Gogi says.

"But—"

"*Forgiven*, Rumi."

Gogi's fur is soft against Rumi's sensitive frog skin. The trembling that took over his body gradually stills and stops. "Gogi. Thank you."

"As long as you didn't just poison me," Gogi says.

"I managed not to," Rumi murmurs.

The hum of Gogi's pulse makes Rumi realize how

rarely he's been in physical contact with his friends, how much his poison skin and intellectual calculations have kept them at a distance. He feels closer to Gogi than he ever has before. And how did it happen? By revealing what he thought was the worst thing about him.

*How wonderful hearts are,* he thinks to himself. *And how very fascinating.*

"Will someone *please* tell me what's going on?" Banu says.

Rumi decides that he should be the one to lead them over the rise and into his home swamp. He can't see anything yet, but the smell is what brings it back first. There's a musty tang, tannins from peat moss and the lush rising currents of rotting vegetation. It's a really wonderful place.

Or was.

As Rumi hops nearer, visions come unbidden to his mind, of downed trees and pulverized froglings, of dead birds sprawled on upturned soil.

"Are you ready for this?" Gogi asks.

"Not really," Rumi chirps back, "but I never could be. We should go forward anyway."

"You should at least ride on my head," Gogi says.

"Yes, that would help," Rumi says.

Gogi lifts him to sit between his eyebrows, and

Sky takes up a position at Gogi's side. With Banu just behind, and Auriel riding along Gogi's shoulders, the friends crest the rise.

The trees are still down, giant ironwoods and figs and monguba all interlocking, forming haphazard triangles over the earth.

But each of those fallen giants has sprouted at least a dozen saplings, their reedy trunks a vibrant yellow-green against the open blue sky. Songbirds soar between them, growing nests in the crannies that have opened up in the ravaged trunks. Tree rats nibble on bracket fungus, beneath the flocks of colorful butterflies flitting between the surfaces of the new growth.

"It doesn't look too bad!" Gogi says.

"Well, that shouldn't be surprising," Sky caws. "Life will always find a way."

"I mean, you did probably slaughter thousands of organisms?" Gogi says. "But the rainforest here seems to be recovering."

"Felling those giant trees opened up a whole new patch of jungle," Sky says, tilting his head. "Some of these saplings will someday be giants, and that wouldn't have been possible without the ancient ones falling."

"It still feels terrible, what I did," Rumi says.

"And that's okay too," Sky says. "But your only option is to accept it and move on. There's no alternative."

"How do you feel, buddy?" Gogi asks.

Rumi considers his emotions. He still feels wretched, but he also feels . . . new. Like back when he'd grown his first legs after spending weeks as an algae-scrounging tadpole. "I think I might eventually get my mind around this whole accepting-my-mistakes thing," he says.

"You've been carrying a lot of weight around," Sky says.

"Yes," Rumi replies. "More than I realized."

Gogi taps his lips. "I mean, if you had stolen food from an elderly anteater and then pushed him into a ditch or something, that would be terrible. But blowing up your home swamp? That could happen to anyone!"

"Monkey logic is very strange, but I can't say I mind it," Rumi says. He stares out at the sunset sky, at the possibilities the coming night might bring. "Thanks, Gogi."

"Might I suggest that we return to my directive feathers?" Sky says. "So we can know what's happened to Mez, Chumba, and Lima?"

Rumi hops right into the air, landing on his back and flipping over before leaping into the air again. "Mez, Chumba, and Lima! Yes, right away. My heart feels plenty strong enough now."

# 11

ALL IS FRANTIC fiery chaos, and Rumi, watching through the memory embedded in Sky's feather strapped to Mez's back, can't figure out anything that's happening. Ferns whip through his view, then the starry sky, then fire, terrible arcs of fire. Mez must be barrel-rolling as she tries to escape the attack, Rumi realizes, and it's sending his vision barrel-rolling right along with her. Finally the sights sort themselves out so that he's following Mez more precisely, low and stealthy against the ground. She slinks between and through a melee of enemies, always on the defensive, avoiding the attacks of giant spiders and frogs, of claws and beaks and fangs.

Rumi feels his belly dropping away, nausea threatening to overcome him. But he forces himself to remain engaged in the swirling images, to watch as Mez avoids death time and again, her extraordinary panther reflexes the only thing keeping her from succumbing to snapping jaws and talons. Rumi wonders why she hasn't used her magic, but then realizes his answer when he sees that Chumba is fighting her own battles, surrounded by a horde of enemies. If Mez went invisible, both sets of opponents would be on her sister.

There's a flash of white, and Rumi realizes that there's a method to Mez's movements—she's running from her cultist enemies, but she's also facing down Mist. With his multiple magical abilities, he will surely be an intimidating opponent in open combat, but Mez harries her way closer and closer to him, risking direct confrontation. Maybe there's something to her thinking—for his part, Mist isn't directly engaging, but instead feinting backward, so he keeps his cultists between him and Mez.

Finally Mez fakes left, then breaks right, joining Chumba at her flank. Without needing a single word of communication, the two sisters streak in formation toward Mist. They're in an open space of moist nighttime air, their cousin backed up against the burial mound. Derli's eyes are wide open, watching in terror and desperate hope as his family wheels around him.

"I challenge you!" Mez gasps. "I challenge you for control."

A boa constrictor had been approaching Mez and Chumba from behind, but at Mez's words it stops, tongue licking the air. Apparently even the boa knows the strict rules of panther life.

One of Mist's ears flicks. He tilts his head.

Lima's voice squeaks down from above. "There must be some other way! Don't do this, Mez!"

Chumba purrs loudly, butting her head against Mez's flank, giving a wordless sister warning.

"Mist," Mez growls. "You know the rules. You must accept my challenge."

"There is nothing in Caldera that I 'must' do," Mist hisses, gaze flicking around his assembled minions. "You have been aiding the daywalkers in destroying our land. The old rules are obviously gone."

"What are you talking about? Why would daywalkers want to destroy the rainforest? And how would they cause that smoke? It's a *volcano*, Mist, all of Caldera is a *volcano*, and it's going to explode. You're here trying to accumulate power when everything's going to be gone, all gone, no matter who's in charge. We need to work together if we want to survive."

The nightwalker cult begins to hoot and murmur.

"How typical," Mist says. "You'll say anything to get your way, to trick nightwalkers into destroying themselves. We are through with the lies of the shadowwalkers and daywalkers! I will not listen to you."

Mez bares her teeth and paws the earth. "Then you don't need to listen to my words. I'm ready to fight."

"Don't be a fool, Mez," Mist says. "I can destroy you in an instant."

"Be that as it may," Mez says. "I will still try to defeat you."

"Let me do the ritual combat instead!" Chumba says.

"No," Mez replies. "This fight is mine."

There's a flash of anger in Chumba's eyes. Rumi remembers hearing about a time when Chumba was furious about Mez's constant need to protect her.

Mist's minions form a circle around Mez and Mist and Chumba and Derli. Rumi can't see Usha, Yerlo, or Jerlo—they must have gone into hiding during the confrontation. "This is a ritual combat," Mez says. "While it is underway, you must promise the safety of Chumba and Derli. By everything that still might bind you to the panther world."

"And me!" squeaks Lima from somewhere in the

branches up above. "Don't forget about my safety! These owls are terrifying."

"Chumba, get Derli out of the ring," Mez says, keeping her eyes locked on Mist's. "These nightwalkers won't hurt you."

Looking at the malevolent eyes of the nightwalker cult that rings them, eerily lit in the firelight, Rumi's not so sure. But he's powerless to say or do anything about it.

Chumba sets her teeth into the scruff at the nape of Derli's neck and awkwardly drags the young panther into the crowd at the edge of the circle. He's young, but too heavy to drag the way she would a pup. The nightwalkers give them a wide berth, watching the turncoat panthers in disgust.

"This fight is to the death, or to submission," Mez growls.

"And once I defeat you, you can never challenge me again."

Mez's tail thrashes. "Or the other way around, cousin."

He rolls his eyes. "Not likely."

"Back to back," Mez says.

Yowling nervously, the scent of pantherfear heavy in the air, the white and calico panthers back up against

each other, tails whipping and entwining. "Three lengths," Mez says.

They stalk away from each other, with Mez counting. "One . . . two . . . three."

The clearing goes still, the assembled animals silent as they watch the adversaries turn and take each other in. Panthers are ambush predators, so each is missing their primary means of attack. Yowling, they circle the burial mound, waiting for one or the other to make the first move.

Neither uses any magic yet. That makes sense to Rumi: how they use their magical powers could be each animal's one surprise move, and surprise is the main source of a panther's combat strength.

As she circles, Mez veers too close to the assembled nightwalkers, and the ocelot snarls and paws her back into the ring. "Don't you dare get close to me, filthy shadowwalker," it says.

Chumba growls. "There's no rule saying that *I* couldn't attack *you*, pussycat," she says.

The ocelot doesn't back off, exactly, but conspicuously licks its paw and looks away.

Mez tries to regain her poise, but she's caught flat pawed by the ocelot's unexpected shove. Her ears flick. Mist takes advantage of the moment to lunge, his open jaws going for her throat. She leaps away, but Mist's long teeth snag her ear, tearing it to the edge. Mez is immediately on the counterattack, rolling onto her back and wriggling forward, extended front claws grasping for Mist, slashing through air and dirt.

She manages to snag his flank with one claw, rolling her cousin onto his side, where she can rake him with her back paws. The force of it is enough to stretch Mist's body out, his cousin's powerful claws gouging red lines along his rib cage. Mist responds by releasing a jet of air from his shoulders, sending Mez sliding across the battleground, dirt and dead leaves flying through the air.

A jet of air? Mist is using Rumi's own magic against Mez!

Then he adds in Mez's magic. Mist blinks out of view.

Terror rims Mez's eyes in white as she looks about the clearing. Then she goes invisible, too.

The nightwalker cult goes silent. Chumba, Derli, and Lima go silent too, all watching as the two invisible panthers face off. Where are they? As the wait goes long, Rumi wonders if maybe one or both panthers have fled. But there is slightly more sound in the area than the motionless spectators can account for, and here and there a leaf moves, or a stick shifts, with no wind to account for it.

As the invisible standoff continues, the nightwalkers shuffle and murmur. Chumba exchanges looks with Lima. *Do we do something?*

Then there's the fireball.

Mez suddenly materializes, her calico fur singed and smoking. She howls in pain and streaks in retreat—but the ring of nightwalkers blocks her. Panicked, she follows their line, looking for an opening, but the nightwalker cult is ruthless in keeping her in the ring, hissing and lunging.

Mist appears, snarling as he approaches Mez, tail thrashing and teeth bared. Mez doesn't have an extra wit to spend on him, rolling in the mud to try to put out her still-flaming fur.

It's too much for Lima. Screeching wordlessly, she darts through the air toward Mez, landing on her shoulder and bringing her mouth to the fur and burned skin beneath, using the magic in her licks to heal her friend even as bat winds up rolling with panther.

The fire on Mez's fur finally goes out, and Lima goes about licking the wounds that riddle Mez's body.

Her entering the fray, though, has broken the rules, provoking gasps of rage from the assembled nightwalkers. They narrow the ring, licking lips and baring teeth as they descend on Mez and Lima. Panic setting her fur on end, Chumba pushes through the crowd and streaks to join her sister. At least they can go out together.

Mez whirls. "No, Chumba!"

It's the opening that Mist needs. He pounces on Mez, rolling her still-sizzling body in the soil. She howls in pain as he pins her, using his sharp claws to press her smoking body into the ground.

Mist holds up a paw, and the cultists stop their inward push. "So much for honor," he snarls down at Mez. "I have defeated you, and on top of that you have broken the panther code. You have lost this fight. You have lost any status you ever had in the panther world."

Mez hasn't noticed Lima yet. Her eyes dart around in confusion, then she notices the bat on her belly. "Oh no, Lima, you didn't."

"You might have died," Lima says quietly. "You're still seriously wounded."

Mez closes her eyes heavily and nods. "But now I . . . I . . ." She can't seem to bring herself to say it.

"I'm sorry, Mez," Lima says.

"You were only trying to help," Mez whispers, before returning her gaze to her cousin.

Lima goes back to her licking.

"Now I may do with you as I will," Mist says, eyes narrowing.

Chumba cowers by her sister as the rest of the night-walkers close in. She tugs Derli near too, and even though his limbs are still bound, simply to be close to his cousins brings tight relief to his features. Through the directive, Rumi can smell the stinking carrion blossoms of the cult as it hems them in.

"Finish it quick," Mez hisses.

"Nothing about this will be quick," Mist says as he takes a step toward them. "I have plenty of use for you. You will be collateral to get the daywalkers to stop their plan to destroy Caldera."

"For the last time," Mez says, "the daywalkers have no such plan. Why would they destroy their own home? That makes no sense."

But Mist's strategy does make sense, Rumi realizes as he watches the cultists shake their heads severely. Their fear has made them fully committed to Mist. By giving them an enemy, he has made them even more beholden to him. It doesn't matter whether the daywalker conspiracy he's talking about is real. It's terrifyingly effective either way.

Mist gestures to a pair of opossums in the tight circle of nightwalker cultists. "Tie up the panthers and the bat. To appease the forces threatening Caldera, to thwart the explosion threatening our way of life, we will bring the shadowwalkers to the center of Caldera. There we will sacrifice them to the volcano. Then the natural order will finally be restored, and Caldera can go back to the way that it was before either of the eclipses."

The small and nimble animals tear down lengths of vine and approach the panthers. Chumba growls menacingly, hackles rising as she bares her teeth and swats at the air. The opossums lose courage, looking to Mist. But it's Mez who speaks next. "Let them do it," she tells her sister through gritted teeth. "We've lost our advantage here. We're at their mercy."

Chumba looks at Mez in shock, but at the sight of her sister's crestfallen expression, she nods. There's clearly no chance of fighting back now—and they're lucky to have their lives for the time being. Even if it's only eventually to be hurled into smoking lava.

Panthers are such regal, powerful creatures—there's something utterly demoralizing about seeing Mez and then Chumba lower their heads, more and more until they are prone on the ground, chins in the mud. Mez has bald patches where Mist's blast hit her hardest, the calico hair matted and melted. Maybe Lima can heal hair? It seems unlikely. The hair doesn't matter in the long run, of course, but it only adds to Rumi's misery at seeing Mez and Chumba brought so low.

"Now tie them," Mist says.

Lima's wings are soon bound around her with rough liana vine. The opossums even bind her little feet. Then they move on to the panthers, wrapping their ankles together with lengths of braided fibers. The opossums tremble as they maneuver, and Rumi suspects they wouldn't have the courage to even attempt what they're doing if it weren't for Mist's presence.

Rumi wants to look away, but he forces himself to watch every motion as his friends are restrained, paw by paw and wing by wing.

A voice intrudes, a voice he knows but that makes no sense here. "Rumi," it says.

Rumi startles. Who is that? Have the nightwalker cultists seen him, perhaps because Mist absorbed some of Sky's divination magic? But no—the voice is Sky's. It's coming from the other side of the divination, where Rumi's real body is.

"Rumi, come back. Please. We need you!"

12

WHEN RUMI LURCHES back into his own body, he
sees that he's still where he was when he opened
the link to the panthers: nestled into the assortment of
logs that the group has collected. Over the course of the
day, the three muscular tapirs have hauled the lumber
toward the beach, carrying Rumi right along with the
mass. Right now, though, the tapirs are in nightcoma,
the logs motionless until the Veil next lifts.

As Rumi removes his finger from Sky's scarlet
feather, he sees a lot more feathers. These aren't directives, though—they're still attached to the bird himself.
Sky's right beside Rumi, squawking at him.

There are words inside Sky's squawks, but Rumi is

too disoriented from his sudden reentry to his own body to understand them. He shakes his head, trying to clear it. "Wait, what? Slow down."

"The explosion!" Sky says. "We thought we had more time than this, but look!"

It's still nighttime, but even so, dawn has somehow started to light up the horizon. It looks normal ahead, in the direction of the ocean, but as Rumi continues to pivot he sees . . . oh, that's definitely not good. Where the volcano is, the black plumes have increased to cover a good third of the sky, the swirling smoke laced in ribbons of red that fade to grays as the airborne embers wink out. The "dawn" isn't from the sun—it's from the flames.

"You said that we'd have two more rises of the Veil before the volcano went out," Sky says.

Rumi wrings his frog hands. "My calculations would indicate that, yes, based on the two-legs' carvings. But I suppose . . . I suppose they weren't predicting this exact scenario, with the ants speeding up the explosion. That's a whole new variable thrown into the equations. I could try to extrapolate new predicted timings from my previous algorithms—"

"Your words get bigger the more nervous you get, have you ever noticed that?" Sky asks, the slightest wink of humor in his voice.

Rumi blinks. "No, I haven't."

Sky tilts his head. "I notice too much sometimes. It's a bit of a curse. Anyway, you don't need to bother recalculating, since it won't change the reality. We have less time than we thought. I scouted the ocean not far from here—we'll be at the beach soon after we get the tapirs up and moving, then we'll need to get this ark together far sooner than we thought."

"And we'll need to gather as many animals as we can."

"We're already a big group. Given the volume of this wood, and the amount of water we must displace to give us enough buoyancy, we can take some more small animals, but I'm afraid that's about it."

"And Mez and Chumba and Lima, once they're back," Sky says.

"And Mez and Chumba and Lima, of course." Suddenly what Rumi learned through the directive comes rushing back to him. "Mez, Chumba, and Lima! Sky, we have to save them! Mist has cultists, and he's used the volcano rumblings to manipulate their fear and gain power, and he's used it to capture the panther sisters. He's going to sacrifice them to the volcano! They need our help."

Even Sky, who usually takes everything in stride, can't keep his beak from dropping open. "This is bad news, indeed. I was afraid that we hadn't seen the last of Mist."

"He received some of each of our magic during the eclipse. It's made him unstoppable. Our friends don't stand a chance."

"We'll talk to Gogi when he wakes up, of course, but I don't see any way we can help right at this moment, especially not with the eruption so much closer than we thought. We have our own crisis here, and even without that we couldn't make it to the panther forest in time to be of use."

"I know, I know," Rumi says, still wringing his hands. "But it doesn't feel good, not at all."

Sky buries his head under his wing. "Believe me, I feel the same way, friend."

The tapir right under Rumi, a young female named Zuza, opens her soft and long-lashed eyes. She sighs, taking in her surroundings, and then the urgency of their situation hits her awakening brain and she staggers to her feet, lifting the whole mass of logs all on her own, in the process sending a surprised Rumi tumbling to the jungle floor. Sky crashes into the branches above.

The tapir blanches when she sees the ruckus she's created. "Oh, sorry!"

The other tapirs are roused from their sleep by the mayhem, and groggily get to their feet. "Zuza," one says, "we talked about this. Wake us, and *then* stand up."

"I know, I know," she says. "I'm sorry. I just get so excited about what the day might bring. Come on, let's go!"

Rumi hops back onto the mass of logs. "Yes, let's go. There were some developments during the night—we have less time than I thought."

"See, you two?" Zuza says. "Listen to that brilliant tree frog. We have to get to work! Chop chop!"

"I don't know if I'd say *brilliant*," Rumi says bashfully as the tapirs lurch into motion. "But it's very kind of you to say so."

"You certainly seem brilliant to me," Zuza says. "I wouldn't have thought there was enough room in a tiny head for so much brain."

"Oh, *stop it*," Rumi says, slapping Zuza's side.

"Is Gogi up yet?" Sky asks.

"Yeah, yeah, I'm up," the monkey calls from above. Gogi makes his way down from the branches where he was napping and starts to pass through the canopy, hand over hand over tail, making his way along the trees. Auriel doesn't seem to ever sleep, but he spent the night in Gogi's nest and now is traveling on his torso, entwined in the strap of the monkey's pouch.

"Mez, Chumba, and Lima are in big trouble," Rumi calls up. "There's not much we can do about it from here, but I'll fill you in once we get to the beach."

"I wish we could do something about it!" Gogi calls as he scampers along a treetop.

"When I left my home to investigate the rumors of resurrection, I thought we were making this pilgrimage just to see Auriel, the Elemental of Light," Zuza says as she lumbers along. "But now we have a new mission. It's been wonderful to meet you shadowwalkers. You've got this reputation for being the heralds of Caldera's doom and everything, but you're actually pretty nice!"

"Heralds of Caldera's doom!" Rumi says. "I say, that's very unfair!"

"Well," Zuza blunders on, "didn't your coming to the ziggurat help release the Ant Queen in the first place? And didn't you just tell me that's what led to the ants eating through the earth's mantle, which brought on this volcanic explosion? For us to experience all this horrible smoke and noise, and then have songbirds flit by every daytime singing about the yellow boa who once was evil . . . you can't exactly fault us for blaming you all!"

"Even if bad things happened," Sky says bitterly, "it was in the service of trying to help. I'd think everyone would be grateful."

"You know eclipse phobia runs deep in the jungle," Zuza says, "and I understand why. Most animals just want things to stay the way they are. 'New' can feel like the same word as 'dangerous,' like those clouds of black smoke."

"A good point," Rumi says. "Maybe every morning should start with some tapir wisdom. You're a lot like Banu." He whirls around on the wood. "Wait, where's Banu?"

"Don't worry. I'm . . . catching up," comes a voice far off in the forest behind them.

Rumi settles back in. "Oh, good."

Gogi calls down from a treetop ahead. "Just go along this next tight pathway between the thickets, then we're at the ocean."

It's a narrow fit for the tapirs, but despite their broad and muscular bodies they're quite agile, and before long they've all reached the other side. Rumi had hopped to a nearby trunk to avoid getting squished during the transition, and hops back into his vantage spot on top of the logs in time to watch the ground rapidly change from wet muddy soil to sand. With the alteration in terrain, the plants dissipate too, turning to low runty succulents instead of the massive trees of the jungle.

There, on the far side, is the blue-gray expanse of the ocean. Just like last time, it mesmerizes Rumi. A long second goes by as he gets lost in contemplating the depths. What creatures might live within its salty reaches? How far into the distance does the water go? Is it infinite, or does it eventually reach more land?

Then his attention is drawn to the hubbub before him: Gogi scampering along the hot sand, trying to keep his feet and hands from burning; Sky wheeling in the air above, cawing out instructions to the tapirs as they haul the wood onto the beach; the rest of the groupies arriving behind; Banu emerging in the distance. Auriel unravels from Gogi and lays himself out on the hot sand, basking in the rare treat of direct sun.

It's definitely no mistake this time: under the open sunlight, Auriel is growing before Rumi's eyes. His whole body shimmers as he elongates.

Rumi can't spend the whole day staring at their strange resurrected companion, though. There's so much to do. He hops onto the beach, then immediately hops back to a piece of wood, blowing on his fingers and toes. It's so hot! The wood is much cooler. But the sun still beats into Rumi's moist skin, enough that he can actually feel it burning and crisping. He creeps under the flap of one of Zuza's broad ears. "Hope you don't mind, but I need some shade."

"Of course, little frog," Zuza says, flaring her ear so it will provide even more shelter. "I'd be happy to. Just direct your voice outward before you chirp loudly or anything."

"I'll be sure to, and thank you very much," Rumi says. He leans out, trying to get everyone in view at once—then, on reflex, uses his air magic to amplify his voice, making a tornado of sound. Everyone startles and goes still at the loud sound from the tiny frog. "Okay, let's move! Tapirs, we need the wood lined up on the beach, from biggest pieces down to the smallest. Then, Banu, we need you to start waterlogging them. Gogi, work with Banu to see the best way to make steam. Let's go, guys, no time to lose!"

Rumi had been expecting just a wisp of amplification, but his voice came out louder than he's ever been able to make it.

His magic is back! And, from the sound of it, stronger than ever before. He whoops and hollers, his friends wincing at the ruckus. "My magic's back, everyone!"

His hands over his ears, Gogi shakes his head. *Too loud!*

As Zuza lumbers into motion, Rumi whispers into her ear. "I'm sorry, was that too loud?"

"WHAT?" she yells back. "I CAN'T HEAR YOU!"

By the time the Veil is about to drop again, they've made substantial progress. Well, "substantial" might be an overstatement. But Rumi knows from his year spent investigating the stones of the ziggurat ruins that sometimes you have to make a big mess before you can start putting everything in order.

He hops between burned-out logs, wet fronds, and exhausted tapirs slumped in the sand, to make his way to Sky. They're the only two really still alert, probably because they're the only two who haven't been doing manual labor all day. The tapirs are worn out, and Gogi and Banu are draped over each other, the capuchin grooming listlessly through the sloth's hair. They haven't had to do any spectacular displays of magic, like they once did fighting the Ant Queen, but they've been using their abilities in small ways all day to shape the wood, and it's tuckered them out.

"My magic," Rumi says, relieved. "I haven't tested the limits, but my wind cramp is gone. I think—I think I might have more power than ever before."

"That's wonderful," Sky says.

Rumi knows he means those words, but all the same the feathers over Sky's eyes are sticking straight out—a sign his friend has something heavy on his mind. "You've still been retaining the transmission from the directive?" Rumi asks.

"Of course," the macaw answers. "We can catch up with our friends as soon as you're ready."

Although Rumi is desperate to know how the panthers and Lima are doing, he's also scared to potentially find out bad news that he can't do anything about. "In a moment," he says. "I wanted to check in with you about the ark preparations first. We're making progress, don't you think?"

"You don't really mean that," Sky glowers. "This is a disaster. Even if we manage to get these curved planks to fit together, they won't be watertight."

"But we have a plan," Rumi sputters. "We're going to put layers of mud in between, and leaves over that, and more woven fronds! It will work! I'm sure of it!"

"I appreciate your optimism." Sky sighs. "We need it."

The way Sky's talking doesn't make Rumi feel so good—like it's all hopeless, but they might as well keep going just to give themselves something to do while the inevitable apocalypse bears down.

"The directive?" Rumi asks, reaching for Sky's feathers.

"I did have a thought first," Sky says, stepping away. "I'm not sure whether I should even bring it up."

"Of course you should!" Rumi says. Then he sees, from the ruffling of Sky's eye feathers, that he was definitely going to tell him, and this has just been Sky's indirect manner of speaking.

"Okay, here goes," Sky says. "I've been thinking about the Cave of Riddles. About the strange forest of perfectly straight trees we saw depicted there, with the rectangles cut into them, with two-legs behind the rect-angles."

"Yes," Rumi said. "The two-legs were getting in those animals with circles for feet, and riding them into another volcano."

"Well, I've been thinking: What if that's the *same* volcano?"

"That seems impossible," Rumi says. "This one is surrounded by a rainforest, and there aren't any two-leg cities around."

"But the two-legs were once here," Sky presses. "We have proof of that—the ziggurat ruins. What if that for-est of straight trees was around here too, only the water rose up around the high mountain, covering the forest and destroying the two-legs as it rose?"

Rumi taps his fingers to his lips as he stares out at the ocean. "So you're saying that those magical decora-tions actually represented something, and now it's all buried under the giant ocean puddle?"

Sky cocks his head. "Yes. I suppose that's what I'm saying."

Rumi stares out at the gray-blue void that he'd been so curious about. Maybe it does hold secrets that could be useful, knowledge to be uncovered—knowledge that might yet save the day. "Their pathway into the volcano could be useful—we could get much farther down to the source of the magma than we were able to by entering the volcano from above."

"Exactly. But the pathway is now—"

"Underwater!" Rumi finishes excitedly. "Though it wasn't underwater in the cave carvings. What a puzzle."

"I thought so," Sky said, fluffing his feathers.

Standing on Sky's claws so that his own soft feet don't get burned by the sand, Rumi takes up a stick and begins to draw diagrams and equations. "Perhaps, if we could only enter the surface at such a trajectory to allow an initial velocity that could overcome the surface tension and propel us at enough acceleration to achieve maximal entry before needing the use of additional propellant mechanisms . . . no, that won't work." He scratches out his work and starts again. "Let's see, if we . . ."

Sky watches admiringly as Rumi speeds through multiple sets of calculations.

Finally Rumi looks up and claps his little frog fingers. "We'll have to delegate the construction of the ark to the tapirs, but I think I've got it! It's going to take every ounce of our magical abilities, each of us."

Sky's eyes light up. "This is great news! Maybe you don't need my divination abilities? Perhaps I could stay behind and supervise the ark construction. Macaws are not especially partial to water."

"I'll need you too," Rumi says. "We'll need whatever your magic can provide for navigation down there."

Sky fluffs his feathers back up. "In that case, I agree to go. Zuza has proven a good worker and planner. We can leave her in charge."

"We shouldn't be gone too long," Rumi says. Then he gulps. "If all goes according to plan, of course."

Sky looks over at Gogi and Banu, slumped together. Gogi's head has been nodding, and before their eyes he falls fully asleep, turning over and falling spread-eagled into the sand, snoring away. "I'm thinking it might take all of our magical powers just to wake up Gogi and Banu."

## 13

BEFORE HE DOES anything else, though, Rumi uses Sky's directive to check on the panther squad. The magic brings him right back into the nightwalker cult's clearing. The hirsuta trees still blaze, but they're less eerie now, because day is fully upon the scene. There is no hushed chanting of Mist's name, no shrill calls for murder and sacrifice. Everyone is in daycoma.

Everyone, that is, except the shadowwalkers Mez and Lima. Even Mist is asleep; at least the magic he wrested from the shadowwalkers didn't also come with their power to cross the Veil. With all their enemies comatose, Mez could easily escape—if she could move. Surrounded by the carrion stench of the nightwalker cult, the shadowwalkers are trussed up, multiple lengths of liana binding ankles and feet. Even Lima's wings have been wrapped tight around her body. She has managed to tip herself over, and by wriggling her body against her bonds, Mez can expose her various gouges and burn wounds to Lima's healing licks.

What happens now? Mez, like Usha, has no option left to challenge Mist's dominance over this area of the jungle. And if Mez, with her combat experience and magical invisibility, wasn't able to defeat Mist, then what chance do any of the others have?

Worst were Mist's words before the rising of the Veil, still rattling around Rumi's mind. The nightwalker cult will make a ruthless march to the volcano, and once there, Mist will hurl his cousins into it.

How is Mez handling the anguish of it? Rumi looks deeper and deeper into her eyes, and suddenly, like submerging into a warm pool, he's right inside her mind. Sky's directive continues to increase in power.

Despite the pain it brings as the thorny vines rub against her fur and flesh, Mez can't help but shudder. *Come on,* Rumi hears her tell herself, *come on. Make a plan. You can come up with something. There's always something.*

*Mez,* Rumi tries to say, *I'm here! I can hear you!* But Mez doesn't seem to react. Apparently Sky's directive hasn't become *that* advanced yet.

For the first time Mez can remember, it all feels truly hopeless. She can't even talk to Chumba about it, because their muzzles too are bound tight by vines—and Chumba is in daycoma. At least Mez can look at her sister. Even though Chumba's eyes are closed, Mez knows her well enough that she can read feelings into her sister's sleeping expression, can imagine the sorts of dreams she's having. In a way, they can share their worry and concern. But what they can't do is make a plan.

*Chumba, I love you*, Mez thinks.

Chumba's closed eyes send the same message back. But there are also thoughts and feelings Mez can't quite put her paw on. The tip of Chumba's tail thrashes. Anger, fear, resolve—determination. Mez raises a singed eyebrow. *What's going on in your mind, sister?*

Chumba's tail continues to slash the air.

Mez narrows her eyes, wondering.

Lima licks them both. Healing, healing.

Mez's legs begin to cramp. She curls and uncurls her paws in an effort to get her blood flowing. It helps a little—that and the tingling numbness that Lima's licking gives her. The bat must be running out of saliva, though; she tucks in, and cuddles against Mez's flank. Mez can't move enough against her bonds to snuggle her chin against the bat, but she hopes the rise and fall of her ribs beneath her fur might give her friend a little comfort.

Mez's worry enters repetitive loops: the welfare of her friends, the looming volcanic explosion, whether Rumi and Sky are able to follow what's happening, and if they've found a way to fix things. But there's nothing she can do about it. There's not even a way to *move*. So she lies there, stewing, her thoughts repeating. Useless.

The Veil begins to drop. The sun's heat slants, then the cicadas build their drone, the sound rising and then falling away, replaced by the insistent buzzing of mosquitoes. Normally Mez's thick fur protects her from them, but though her wounds from her battle with Mist are mostly healed, much of her skin is tender, hairless, and exposed.

There's nothing she can do to keep the mosquitoes off. All she can do is watch them suck her blood. It's not helping her mood.

As the sky darkens, the nightwalker cult begins to stir. The animals unsteadily get to their feet and talons and bellies, fixing their captives with glares that somehow manage to be both groggy and menacing. As the rest awaken, they add their glares, and the grogginess fades. Mez gulps. Now it's just the menacing part.

Mist is the last to rise, yawning widely to expose

his long canines, and kneading the earth with his claws before turning his gaze to the captives. "I see you're still here, cousins."

Lima makes a squeak of protest.

"And the annoying little healing bat, too," Mist says.

Mist pads toward the bound panthers, leans down, and places his jaws right against Mez's face. His foul breath rolls over her. "Good dropping of the Veil to you, my discolored cousin," he says.

Mez wouldn't have answered, even if she could. She holds tight, watching Mist with wide eyes. He circles the restrained panthers again, stepping between and through their intertwined legs and tails. When he comes to Chumba, he leans down. Mez expects him to speak to Chumba, but instead he places his jaws around Chumba's neck. He clamps down.

Chumba sputters and hisses, her eyes wide with fear.

Mist doesn't let go. "I could close my jaws right now," he says, his words muffled, "just a little bit more would be strong enough to break your neck. But I'm choosing not to. I want you to know that."

Chumba sputters more.

Mez becomes enraged, muscles cording against her bonds, tail thrashing so hard it slams the ground with audible thumps. She hisses, but she can't make any words against the bonds binding her muzzle shut.

Chumba's eyes go wider still, then her body goes limp.

The assembled nightwalkers had been making bloodthirsty murmurings before, but now they begin to hiss in alarm. "This is not the time," hoots one of the owls. "They are to be sacrificed! It is their deaths that will stop the volcano! It is their deaths that will save Caldera! This is what you promised!"

Mist nearly snorts at that. But when he looks at Chumba's unmoving body, fear enters his expression. "I didn't mean to kill her, just to scare her," he says. He places a forepaw against his cousin's rib cage, to see if she's still breathing.

The other owls join the first in a chorus of "Not yet! Not yet!"

Cursing under his breath, Mist extends a claw and slashes the cord binding Chumba's mouth.

She gasps in air, nostrils flaring in panic.

Then she abruptly stops. Improbably but unmistakably, a smile crosses her features. "Thank you for releasing my muzzle, Mist," she says.

Confused, Mist hisses. He wheels, looking at his cultists, then back at his cousin.

"I challenge you," Chumba says. "I challenge you for control."

Mist snorts. "You have got to be kidding."

Chumba lets out a low growl. "I promise you that I am not."

"Your sister, who has magical powers when you have none—and four working paws, I might add—tried to fight me and failed. Usha, who is stronger and more experienced than any of you, tried and failed. You think *you* will succeed where they didn't?"

"Yes," Chumba says, a hint of hesitation entering her expression.

Mez strains against her bonds, beaming out a message to her sister: *Don't do this. He will kill you.*

Chumba pointedly turns to face away from Mez, so she can look at Mist—and only Mist—directly. "Let the battle begin, cousin," she says.

Mist bristles. "Right now?"

"Yes," she says.

Mist snorts, then walks a few lengths away to the burial mound. "Same arena as before, then."

"Yes," Chumba says. "I'll just need . . . you need to release me from these bonds first."

"Is that so?" Mist scoffs. "I'm not sure. Maybe I'll decide to release you. Maybe not."

"You know the panther code requires a fair start," comes a voice from the other side of the clearing.

The nightwalker cult, the panthers, and Mist turn

to see Aunt Usha step between two hirsuta trees. She moves forward only enough to come fully into view, then stops, wary. Her movements are rigid and pained, but even so are not without her usual stateliness. Rumi can see why she's stayed near the hiding spot—Jerlo quivers in fear just within the camouflage of the fern. "You must accept Chumba's challenge, and it must be a fair combat," Usha says. "You may no longer be my son, but you are still a panther. Some ties still bind you."

Mez's eyes flit between Usha and Chumba and Derli. *Did you all know this would happen?*

Mist looks pained for a moment at Usha's words. Then he gets control of himself and rolls his eyes. "Yes, fine, though Chumba going up against someone as powerful as *me* can never be considered a fair fight."

"You have broken all the other bonds that animals might have with one another," Usha says. "I'm glad that at least you haven't gone against your very pantherness."

Mist gets an odd, distant look on his face. "I have not broken the panther code, Mother. My defeat of you was not against the panther code. My defeat of Mez was not against the panther code—she was the one who broke it, by seeking help from her ally. I will fight Chumba, don't you worry. I will destroy her, if need be."

"Release me and we'll see about that," Chumba says

through gritted teeth.

Mist extends a claw to slash through one bond, then another, then the next. Once Chumba can, she gets to all fours, wincing as blood flow returns to her legs and paws. Mez—and therefore Rumi—can imagine the tingly feeling, as if she's dropped from a height.

"Ready, cousin?" Mist says.

"Give me . . . a moment," Chumba says, wobbling.

Mez strains against her own bonds, whimpering through her closed muzzle. If only Mist would release *her*, she'd make Chumba stop, she'd throw herself at her cousin again, she'd offer her own sacrifice to keep her sister alive. That's how it has always worked, Mez stepping in, doing the extraordinary to keep Chumba safe . . .

. . . until now. *Maybe that's why this is happening,* Mez thinks, trying to peer into Chumba's eyes even though her sister steadfastly refuses to look at her. *Chumba is stepping into the role of protector, even if it means the end of her.*

Chumba closes her eyes even tighter, girding herself. She tilts her head this way and then that, spine crackling. Finally she speaks. "I'm ready."

She doesn't *look* ready. Rumi can feel the worry rippling through Mez's mind, can see concern wrinkling Usha's usually serene and expressionless face. Her aunt doesn't interfere, though. Even if it's an unlikely one, Chumba represents the panthers' last hope.

Chumba approaches the burial mound and turns, ears drooping and teeth bared as she pants in the nighttime heat. Mist pads his way over and turns, allowing his tail to entwine with Chumba's, just like it had done with Mez's a short while before.

White and calico panthers, snapping and whipping, each panther letting out low yowls as it squares off. Rumi's gotten so used to his panther companions that it comes as some surprise to realize all over again how powerful they are, how muscled their jaws and legs, how thick their flanks and backs. A panther's jaws can puncture the head of an alligator, and seeing these two in battle preparations, it's not hard to see why.

"It's been good knowing you, cousin," Mist says.

Chumba doesn't reply, except to say, "Count. Off."

Their tails unlock as they pace forward with each of Mist's counts. "One . . . two . . . three!"

Both whirl, teeth bared, feinting and retreating as they gauge the distance between them. They're too far apart for either to lunge yet, so they begin to circle, hackles up as they pass around the burial mound. Chumba starts making a terrible keening noise, loud and desperate, unlike anything Rumi has ever heard from her. Is it fear? Is it intimidation? It's hard to know. Rumi certainly wouldn't want to face off against her, not on any cycle of the moon, but Mist is bigger, and has magic on his side.

He plants his four limbs heavily in the soil and lowers his head, jaws open. Instead of howling, though, he emits a burst of air—Rumi's own power. It roars through the clearing, flattening ferns and bushes, sending Chumba skidding in the dirt. Mist takes advantage of the opportunity to leap, disappearing in midair as he does. Chumba looks up, startled into stillness before her reflexes bring her dodging. She chooses her direction wisely, as a thicket on the other side of where she was crackles and breaks as Mist's body slams into it. He goes visible, whirling and hissing. "You won't be so lucky next time," he growls.

Chumba doesn't bother to answer. She continues her keening, teeth bared. Mist appears unruffled by the unnerving yowling except for one ear, which flicks in irritation. He goes invisible again.

Mist's going invisible got Mez springing into fast motion, but that's not Chumba's response. She goes stock-still, nose in the air. She closes her eyes. Mez gasps, the sound of it strangled against her gag. *What is Chumba doing?*

But of course—vision isn't useful anymore, so Chumba is focusing on her other senses. The calico panther's fur ripples as she enters high-alert mode. There's a popping sound, and then an arc of flame shoots in from the right. It fills Rumi's and Mez's vision, becoming all they can see or think about, but Chumba uses the sound to figure out where to spring into the air again. Eyes still shut, she leaps over the flame. This time she doesn't dodge to the right or left, but instead soars above and *toward* the source of the popping—invisible Mist.

Chumba rolls. Her jaws snap around empty air, her back claws rake the earth—until they strike something . . . that yowls in pain. Mist materializes, belly up, fighting against his cousin's snapping jaws. He sends out a buffet of wind that pops Chumba up into the air, but as soon as she's landed, her jaws are back at Mist, snapping and snarling. She uses her pawless foreleg strategically to pin Mist's chest against the earth while her foreclaw scrapes his shoulder and throat.

Mist isn't out of tricks yet, though. His fur smolders and then blazes, causing Chumba to yelp even as she keeps up the attack. Rumi knows from his experiences around Gogi's fire that Mist is probably immune to the effects of his own magic, so when the sickly sweet smell of burning fur enters the clearing, he knows that Chumba is getting injured as she presses the onslaught. She finally relents, limping and cringing.

Now it's Mist's turn to go on the attack. Fury contorts his features as he goes into full assault mode, hissing in rage as he snaps his teeth at his cousin. Chumba rapidly backs up, keeping her eyes trained on Mist even as she retreats. She's soon snarled in the line of watching nightwalkers, who jeer at her and press her back into the makeshift arena. She skirts the line while Mist stalks toward her.

He slaps the ground with a paw, sending a line of fire along the soil, arcing toward Chumba. She leaps away, but before she even lands Mist has sent out another line of fire, speeding to her new position. Chumba leaps again, only just getting her tail clear of the flame this time. She must be getting tired; how long can she keep this up?

Mist sends out stream after stream of fire, Chumba dancing through the air as she dodges and rolls. She'll never get the initiative back at this rate, and will just continue dodging until her body fails her. Unless . . .

Yes, Rumi's suspicion is correct: once again, Chumba's making her way *toward* Mist. Though dodging side to side, she's also working her way back up to him, one panther-length at a time. Intent on the attack, Mist doesn't seem to notice, snarling and thrashing as he sends out stream after stream of flame.

"Are you ready to give up yet, cousin?" he calls.

Chumba doesn't answer, just continues to dodge and roll.

Mez struggles violently against her bonds. Rumi plainly reads the expression on her face: *Just ask for mercy, Chumba!*

For a moment, the first time since the combat started, Chumba goes still. She howls and then—*whoosh*—she's flying through the air, up and over the latest streak of flame Mist sent out, down right onto Mist himself. She locks her jaw around the back of his neck, pressing him into the mussed earth.

Focused on producing his streaks of fire, Mist is taken totally unawares. This time Chumba's not giving him the chance to muster up more flame. She bites down hard, and Mist's eyes go wide, rimmed white. He chokes and shrieks into the soil.

The shadowwalker cult gasps, animals shuffling from one side to the other, looking at one another: *What do we do?* Mez puts a paw in front of her face, in shock. Derli hides his face.

*Will Chumba kill Mist?*

The white panther writhes and thrashes, but Chumba won't let go, scrunching her eyes shut against the pain as desperate claws rake her belly and backside. Nothing will make her release this time.

"Say 'mercy,'" she hisses through her locked jaws.

Mist doesn't respond, just squirms and begins to smolder.

Chumba clenches her grip tighter. "No fire. You die the moment you make fire. Now say it."

From across Sky's directive, Rumi can hear the awful sound of neck bones creaking, beginning to splinter.

"Agh!" Mist screams. "I give up! Mercy!"

Chumba releases her jaws and flops onto the earth, flat on her back. There's not even enough energy left in her to get into a defensive position.

An astonished pall descends over the nightwalker cult. They look to one another, baffled. *It was not supposed to go this way.*

Mist is prone on the ground, gasping against the soil. No, not gasping—sobbing. Great tears fall from his eyes, and his belly heaves. He can't seem to get in any air, is howling too quickly. Chumba wearily gets to her feet, places a tentative paw against Mist's ribs. "You're hyperventilating. Take deep breaths."

"Get away from me!" Mist shrieks, shoving against Chumba, missing her entirely in his misery.

She steps back, forepaw up to show she means no harm. "I'm not going to hurt you," she says. "The battle is over."

Chumba steps to Mez and Derli and deftly slices through their bonds. The panthers get to their feet, shaking out sore limbs and joints. Usha and Jerlo join them, limping across the clearing.

Sobbing and howling, Mist staggers to all fours and takes in his family, lined up against him. He stares at the cult members, who refuse to look into his eyes, shifting their baffled gazes across the ground. "You cheated," he accuses Chumba.

"How did I cheat?" she asks, a look of genuine confusion on her face.

"I don't know, but you must have. I defeated Mez. I couldn't lose to you."

"If you'd been paying attention, you'd have seen that Chumba was always the more powerful fighter of the two of us," Mez says. "With or without magic."

"She doesn't even have both forepaws," Mist spits.

"Which led to your underestimating me, which led to your defeat," Chumba says sharply. She looks about her. "I am now in control of this region, and the panthers who wish to live here will do so only with my authorization. This cult is disbanded, and I will not permit it to come back together. You may not consort with my cousin again. Go! Back to your homes!"

The nightwalker cultists stare back at her balefully.

"If you obey me, I will rule as panthers always have, and not interfere directly in your lives," Chumba says. "Go now, and run. Don't make me regret my choice."

"You heard her. Go!" Aunt Usha snarls, drawing up high on all fours, glowering.

The nightwalker cultists waste no time in disappearing into the shadows.

Mist's breathing slowly returns to normal. He faces his family, the panthers he grew up with, looks at them one by one. "So this is it," he says finally. "You're exiling me."

"Mist," Mez says, her tone neutral. She cuts her eyes to Chumba before continuing. "We can't forgive you for what you did here, for what you were about to do to Derli, Chumba, and me. But the volcano underneath the rainforest is about to erupt. All of Caldera—including you, including us—will be destroyed when it does. You have been gifted with magic by the lunar eclipse, magic that might help us stave off the explosion. Will you join your powers with ours? Will you help us find an answer? What's at stake is greater than any petty family power struggles."

Shoulders slumped in misery, Mist looks at his mother, his cousins, his siblings.

He considers his words.

His ruined lips pull back from his teeth, and his jaws clench so hard that Rumi can hear his teeth shiver and grind. Finally he speaks. "No. It was you who ruined me. I will never work with you."

With a howl of rage, Mist turns invisible.

His family goes still, noses in the air, trying to detect any sign of him. But it's impossible.

Mist is gone.

Within mere minutes, there's no sign left that the night-walker cult has ever existed. They've all skulked off into the brush or soared through the night. Lima watches them go, indignantly waving her scrunched wing at the sky. "Cowards! Stay here and fix the mess you made!" She looks at the mussed earth, shaking her head in outrage. "Look at this, leaving their gross rotting flowers everywhere. Did they even think about who would have to clean it up after? No, of course not. Sometimes I'm embarrassed to be a nightflyer."

It's Lima's first moment up and about, after some emergency licking of Mez's and Chumba's various wounds. She takes a long draft of water from a nearby pond to replenish herself, then returns to licking. "Wow, you two panthers take up a lot of bat saliva, you know that?"

The two sisters don't seem quite to know what to say to that. "We're very grateful for that bat slobber," Mez finally says.

"Saliva," Lima huffs.

"Sorry, saliva."

Ever since Derli was freed and the triplets reunited with their mother, Usha hasn't let them out of her sight. Though well beyond their cub stage, the panthers allow themselves to be licked and groomed and cuddled. Now, though, with effort, Usha gets to all fours, taking in the starry night sky, the waving branches of tree silhouettes, the lights of the click beetles darting through the air. "I'll never be back at my full strength," Usha says, turning to her family. "But at least order has returned. This part of the rainforest is back to our family's control."

"Mist *was* our family," Jerlo moans.

"Don't tell me you miss him," Yerlo says sharply.

"Enough. We will say his name no more," Usha commands. Though Usha would never admit such things, Rumi thinks he can see wistful regret in her expression. She used to dote on Mist. In a way, she's responsible for his sense of ruthless entitlement.

Chumba shocks Rumi by hissing, standing right before her aunt and baring her teeth in defiance. "No, we *will* say his name. Trying to ignore Mist before only gave him more power, gave him full freedom to manipulate the nightwalkers' fear. Mist is our family, whether we like it or not, and his actions are our responsibility. He has chosen the selfish path, time and time again, but I hope there's some good left in him. If he shows his face here again, you will bring him to me and we will face him, hear him out, and punish him as necessary."

Usha hisses back. "Chumba, you may have won this battle, but I will not tolerate your—"

"I *did* win the battle, Aunt Usha, and we both know precisely what that means," Chumba says. "One panther is to be in charge of each region of Caldera. The panther in charge of this region is now me. I do not intend to be a harsh ruler. Hopefully most animals won't even know that I'm in charge. I will welcome your input if big decisions have to be made. But how we move forward regarding Mist is my decision alone to make."

For a long moment, Usha stares coolly at Chumba, her claws kneading the earth. Then, after a long blink, she nods and lays herself out on the ground, belly up. The submissive position.

Mez looks between the two of them in shock, then uses her paw to close her gaping mouth.

Chumba looks at Mez and Lima. "Now that I'm in charge, here is where I need to stay. What do you two intend to do?"

Mez's eyes tear up. "I want to stay, and help you and Usha and the triplets when disaster comes. If this volcano . . . if it's the end of everything, I want to die by your side. But our best chance still rests with Sky, Rumi, Gogi, and Auriel. They might have come up with some way to prevent the eruption, and if there's any way that we can do that, then I . . . well, I . . ."

Chumba nods. "Of course. Say no more, sister. I understand."

Lima squeaks. "I want to stay here with the panthers too. But you're right, Mez."

Mez's eyes look into the distance, then back at her sister with a desperate gleam. "I'll miss you so much. Chumba, if this all . . . if the shadowwalkers don't succeed and this is the end for some reason . . ."

"Just succeed," Chumba says. "If you succeed, we only have to say good-bye for a few days."

"I love you so much," Mez says.

"I love you too," Chumba says. "Now, go. Fast. Go and don't look back."

Mez blinks against the tears in her eyes, then nods at Usha and the triplets in turn.

"Yerlo, escort Mez and Lima to the edge of our territory and then return here," Chumba says. "In case any of that nightwalker cult tries to regroup, I don't want them giving our rainforest's best hope any trouble."

Yerlo nods and then stalks off after Mez, Lima hanging upside down under her chin.

Right before she passes out of sight, Mez does look back, once. Soaks in the sight of her sister. Then she's gone into the night.

Rumi releases the directive. He keeps his eyes closed

for a long second, so that the transition back to the beach isn't too sudden. He lets the magnitude of Chumba's new authority wash over him.

Then he opens his mouth to whoop in glee. "They're coming home! Mez and Lima are on their way!"

AURIEL IS AGITATED. His sunshine-yellow color has turned more mottled, like a fiery late afternoon sun stained through by the beginnings of sunset. Oranges and reds pass through him as he slithers and licks the air, circling the makeshift raft while the shadowwalker boys and their daywalker allies work on it. Rumi watches Auriel twine himself through the fibers and leaves and mud.

Gogi has been using his fire to harden the mud on the sides of the escape raft, to make them waterproof. He takes a break, though, collapsing against a palm tree at the edge of the beach. Rumi plops his way across to him, sitting on Gogi's knee and using his magic to send breezes over the overheated capuchin.

"Thanks, buddy," Gogi says. "I'm so glad you got your air power back. This cooling wind is a total life changer."

"Have you noticed Auriel lately?" Rumi asks between gusts.

"You mean the weird colors and the frantic slithering? Yep, I noticed. Sort of hard not to."

The air flashes red as Sky lands beside them. "Yes, I've been wondering about it, too. I'm not as concerned about the color as his change in behavior. Anxiety seems out of character for him."

"I'm not sure what would count as *in* character for a magical boa constrictor who's been brought back from the dead," Gogi observes.

"Fair enough," Rumi says.

"If only he could talk to us," Sky says. "Then we might be able to know what's on his mind. We'll watch him closely. That's all we can do. Oh, wait. Would you look at that!"

"Look at what—oh!" Rumi says. Auriel has threaded his way down to the water and is making little forays into the surf.

"Can he even swim?" Gogi asks.

"I don't know," Rumi says. "I've seen many snakes swim before. I certainly hope Auriel can, since he's going right into the water."

"Should we be doing something?" Gogi asks. "In case he drowns?"

"I can swim!" Zuza the tapir calls from where she's constructing the far side of the raft. "You might not think it to look at me, but I'm pretty good. Want me to go in and start a rescue?"

"That's okay!" Gogi calls back. "You just keep on hauling lumber, please!"

"Okay!" she says cheerfully, the beach soon filling with the clamor of logs striking logs.

Auriel ventures into the surf, then looks pointedly back at the shadowwalkers before heading back into the surf again. Rumi sighs. "I think I know what this means. Auriel wants us to start our underwater adventure now."

"I hadn't thought Auriel would be coming with us down there," Sky says.

"I'm actually sort of glad to have his company," Gogi says. "For a reptile that once tried to kill me and now doesn't say a word, I'm pretty fond of him. And apparently he's fond of us."

"I wouldn't say he's fond of us," Sky says. "My guess is we're useful to him, that's all."

"We can always trust you to have the most cynical interpretation," Gogi says, rolling his eyes.

"Hello . . . everyone?" comes Banu's voice from the

far side of the craft. "Are you all seeing . . . that Auriel's gone swimming?"

"Yes!" Rumi croaks. "Are you ready to go?"

"I've been practicing . . . my skills," Banu says. "I think . . . I'm ready!"

"Not sure if 'I think I'm ready' is what I want to hear before diving into the sea," Gogi grumbles.

"Imagine everything that we'll discover!" Rumi says rapturously. "There could be all sorts of life down there, plants that we've never seen or heard of—"

"Monsters and beasts all ready to eat us," Sky adds.

Gogi looks between them. "I'm feeling very complicated emotions about you two right now," he says.

Rumi bounces along the hot beach, gasping whenever the sand sears his sensitive hands. He douses them in the water at the ocean's edge, but the salt only makes the burns hurt more. While he debates whether to stick his hands back in, a wave bowls him over. He sputters. Now the salt is stinging his entire body. Sometimes it's hard to be a frog, there's simply no way around it.

Something strong grips Rumi's body, then he's lifted to safety. Rumi's surprised to discover that it's Sky's beak that plucked him free, not Gogi's hand or tail. Sky gently lays him out on a piece of dried seaweed, cooler than the surrounding sand. "Thanks!" Rumi says, worrying his hands as he stares into Sky's mysterious black eye. "Sometimes I get too excited to start, and it gets me in danger."

"I do not tend to get overexcited, but I can imagine what it might feel like," Sky says. "I'm very happy to rescue you."

Gogi's standing in the seawater, looking brave and looking miserable. Rumi knows how much the capuchin hates getting wet, and right now he's standing on his legs, arms awkwardly over his head, gasping and yelling each time the ocean water gets higher on his body. "Let's hurry up," he says. "I'm ready to be done and drying off already."

"On it," Banu says. Rumi looks around, trying to see where his friend is, unable to know for sure because of the roar of the waves. Then he sees it—Banu is swimming. He's surprisingly agile, his long-clawed arms cutting cleanly through the waves. Banu closes his eyes for a moment, then suddenly he's standing on the ocean bottom. The water has parted around him in a neat U, dark seafloor exposed all the way up to the beach, two crabs blinking in surprise at the sudden sunshine before scuttling off and disappearing into the wall of water.

"Wow," Rumi says.

Banu looks around, claws on his hips, proud of himself. "Pretty nifty, huh?"

"Very!" Rumi says, clapping.

Gogi takes a step forward, then shrieks when his tender belly gets wet. "Could you move a little closer to shore?" he asks.

"Oh . . . of course," Banu says. "Sorry."

The sloth crawls toward the shore. Once the circle of open space joins the beach, Gogi steps in. "Ooh," he says. "Wet sand feels very nice on blistered feet."

Rumi hops to join him, and lets out a sigh of relief. "Agreed! Even though it's a little too salty for my tastes."

Auriel swims through the waves, easily surfing the ocean current before popping out of the wall of water to wriggle along the wet ground.

"Looks like Auriel's decided he's definitely coming with us," Gogi says.

While Sky struts his way into the circular clearing, Rumi looks toward the line of palms that separate the beach from the jungle. "I'd hoped Mez and Lima might be back by now," he says.

"They'll be right here waiting for us when we return," Gogi says. "I'm sure of it." Rumi appreciates his friend's hopeful words, but can't help but notice the worry drawing the monkey's lips tight.

Rumi creeps toward the wall of water, where a school of fish stares back at him, seemingly as astonished as Rumi is by this strange turn of events. Banu takes a step farther, which causes the open space of air to move too, surprising one of the fish. One moment it's floating in the water, and the next it's plopped to the ground, gasping. Rumi gets his sticky fingers around the fish's glistening scales, then hurls it into the wall of water. It looks back, blinks a fishy thank-you, then speeds off into the sea.

"Are you all . . . ready?" Banu asks.

"We are," Rumi says. "Just think of it—we're about to uncover more mysteries of the two-leg civilization. I couldn't be more ready!"

"Rumi's got enough enthusiasm for the rest of us," Gogi says, eyeing the wall of ocean water dubiously.

"If it still exists, that two-leg tunnel we saw in the carvings would pass right into the volcano beneath Caldera," Sky says. "This could be the solution to all of our problems."

"Yes, yes, I know," Gogi says. "That doesn't mean I have to be comfortable with going under the ocean."

"Bye, Zuza!" Rumi calls.

"So long, guys, have fun!" Zuza responds from far up the beach.

"Not likely," Gogi says, arms tight around his chest.

"Here we go," Banu says. He crawls away from the beach, the bubble moving with him, centered around the sloth. The companions keep as close to Banu as possible. Rumi rides on his shoulder, Sky struts alongside,

Gogi hobbles behind, so close to Banu that he's clutching him hard around the backside, like a baby monkey riding its mother. Auriel is the only fearless one, patrolling the edges of the circle, alternating tastes of air and saltwater.

As the seafloor slopes down, the water appears to rise around them, soon towering high overhead. It begins to crawl into the air over them, water flowing and spreading so it finally meets right above Banu, so that they are traveling along the ocean floor in a perfect hemisphere of open space. It gets dark like a den, too, as the seawater above chokes out the sunlight. It's dusky for a while, and then the light goes out entirely, as if the Veil has dropped.

Gogi readies a fire on his tail, like he's done before when nightwalking. The air immediately turns smoky. Before anyone needs to tell him to, Gogi drops the flame. "Sorry, guys!"

It turns out to have been unnecessary. As it gets darker, Auriel brightens his sunshine yellows, giving the magical hemisphere of air the radiance of a cool dawn.

The seafloor beneath them changes, turning craggy. The rocks are slimy, often covered in green plants, and strange sharp white things that Rumi witnesses sometimes extending a little frond. "I wonder if they use those to catch their food," Rumi ponders aloud. His friends are too distracted, though, to be much interested in his intellectual investigations.

It gets chillier and chillier as they go, and the companions find themselves huddling tighter together, not for safety as much as for warmth. Gogi adds just enough fire magic to his fur to heat and dry it, and the hemisphere fills with the pleasant, yeasty smell of drying animal.

Rumi wishes he could pause every few feet, to observe and examine and study. The seabed isn't perfectly flat, for one thing, and not even all that sandy! The ground is hard, and covered with rocks and unfamiliar creatures. A spiny thing that looks like a giant cockroach stares back at them with eyes on the ends of stalks. A blobby creature tumbles to the ground when the wall of air hits it. Sky and Banu walk over it just fine with their claws, but when Gogi steps on it he howls in pain, sending Rumi tumbling down to the ground—luckily not onto the strange stinging creature. Once Banu passes by, the stinging blob lifts back up into the ocean, floating off into the watery dark.

"Fascinating," Rumi says.

"Painful," Gogi corrects.

At first Rumi looks forward to Banu's frequent breaks, since he can further explore the rubbery plants of the seafloor. But as they continue down and Auriel's eerie light feels chillier and chillier, even he wishes they could get on with it, so they could be back on land as soon as possible. There's so much water above them now, enough to drown them many times over. Or maybe it would crush them before it could drown them? Hmm! Rumi does some fast calculations in his head. Yep, it would crush them first.

He shivers and draws even nearer Gogi's fire-warmed fur. The tireless pursuit of knowledge definitely has its downsides.

The seafloor gets even rockier, then the rocks rise steeply enough that Banu, even with his long curved claws, can't get a grip.

"Wait, everyone," Sky says as he closes his black eyes. He opens them. "From my memory of the map in the Cave of Riddles, we're entering the strange zone of vertical trees, or whatever is left of them. Once we're over this blockade and through the vertical trees, we'll get to the tunnel that heads into the side of Caldera, which might lead to the magma source."

"Okay," Rumi says, shivering as he peers upward, froggy hands on his hips. "We have to get over this rocky cliff, then, don't we?"

"Let me give this one more shot," Banu tells Rumi. "Wait down here until I'm sure I won't fall." After the tree frog hops off his back, Banu carefully selects two handholds, wedges his foreclaws into them, and pulls. Then he wedges his back claws into two cracks and heaves himself farther before selecting two spots for his foreclaws, higher up. "It's . . . working!" he calls down excitedly. "I'm . . . climbing!"

Rumi stares up. "That's great, Banu!" He flicks his back legs against a strange tickling sensation, but it's right back, even stronger. He flicks again, but in response he's suddenly lost in cold, dark sea. "Help!" he shouts, or tries to shout, only inhaling saltwater instead.

Then there's a hand darting in from the darkness, gripping him around the midsection and pulling him back into the dryness and light. A monkey finger pushes his belly, and Rumi lets out a fountain of ocean water. Once his panic fades, Rumi's expression settles on Gogi's worried expression. "What's the matter?" Rumi asks.

"You okay, buddy?" Gogi asks.

Rumi nods. "Water's not as scary to a frog as it is to a monkey. But I'm still very glad you rescued me. Now, um, you should consider rescuing yourself."

Gogi looks down and yelps when he sees that the dark seawater is up to his ribs, and continuing to rise. "Why is this happening?" he asks, thrusting Rumi over his head to keep him out of the water for as long as possible.

"Banu's moving upward, and he's bringing the water-free zone up with him!" Rumi says. "Hurry."

"On it," Gogi says. He's a magnificent climber, scrambling his way up the slick rocks until he's beside Banu, the water-air boundary safely below. They're surrounded by cool, buttery, shifting yellows as Auriel snakes through the crannies alongside them.

"All present and accounted for?" Sky asks, flapping nearby, sending gusts of cold air over them as he flutter-lands against the wet kelpy rocks.

Rumi does a quick head count of the shadowwalkers in the bubble. "Yep! All present." They're not looking in great shape, though. Gogi's breathing shallowly, eyes darting about in low-level terror; Sky's feathers are wet, which must be impeding his ability to fly, not that there's anywhere he can go; Rumi can feel his skin stinging everywhere from the salt—that mouthful of seawater didn't exactly help, either; Banu's eyes are half-lidded—he's clearly getting tired from the expenditure of magic. Auriel's the only one who seems unaffected by their strange journey. He weaves along the rocks, tasting the air, inscrutable.

After resting a moment, Banu lurches back into motion. "All right, Banu," he encourages himself. "Up . . . and over!"

Gogi scrambles to keep up as Banu disappears over

the crest of the rock, then scrambles even harder when Banu grunts and falls on the far side, taking the bubble of open space with him.

Hand over foot over tail, Gogi just manages to keep ahead of the wall of water behind them, bringing Rumi along for the tumbling, freewheeling ride. They land on a bed of kelp. Between and under the slippery leaves is a strange surface—it's somehow both rough and soft, flecks of jet black within the rubble. Rumi runs his sensitive fingers and toes over it. "Organic composition, but a tightly bonded mixture that I've never encountered before. I wonder if this is something created by the two-legs, perhaps, as a way to make their vertical trees. Do you think we could stay here for just a little while, so I could determine more of this substance's properties?"

There's no answer from his companions. Their focus is trained upward.

A strange corner juts into the bubble, just at the edge of its circumference. It's the edge of one of the two-legs' vertical trees. Auriel seems especially intent on it, lacing his way forward along the seafloor, before he dips his head into the wall of water. His radiance passes through the membrane and into the ocean, lighting up the hemisphere surrounding them. Now they can see a few feet into the gloom of the surrounding depths, ominous shapes lurking in the dark.

"Are those . . ." Gogi asks.

"—those are the vertical trees from the carvings in the Cave of Riddles," Sky announces. "We're in the home range of the two-legs."

"Right," Gogi says, letting out a long breath. "I didn't think those were tall monsters looming over us, nope. I'm super brave, we all know that, it's all good."

"Could you push the water back even farther?" Rumi asks Banu.

"There's a lot . . . of pressure," Banu says. "But since we're not moving . . . I think I can manage it." His expression scrunches as he reaches deep into his magic.

Slowly the radius of the bubble pushes back farther, and farther.

Once it's gotten far enough, they all know precisely where they are.

They draw even closer together, awed into silence.

15

GREAT HUSKS OF hollowed-out trees rise through the depths, so tall that they nearly break the sun-marbled surface. They're festooned in broad swaths of kelp and seaweed, every surface covered in the little sharp white things Rumi noticed earlier, but also in larger structures—bony projections, many of them iridescently colored. Pinks, blues, greens, and oranges. They emerge from the vertical trees like horns, projecting into the open space above the companions' heads. Are they plants? Motionless animals? Rumi isn't sure.

Each colored horn is covered in tiny life-forms. Bony fans tickle the air, wafting back and forth even though there is no breeze. There are pulsing tentacles, grouped together like a succulent plant, but these too are moving in the motionless open air. "Are they surprised by us?" Rumi wonders. "I wonder what they're feeling. If anything." It's been the puzzle of his life: how does he know what *anyone* is feeling?

There's no answer to his questions from his friends. Rumi sees their attention is drawn to the seafloor, where a giant beast is thrashing, not more than a thousand frog-lengths away. It's a hairless and muscular fish, much bigger than even the boto they met a few weeks before. Its powerful tail thrashes back and forth (the boto's moved up and down, Rumi recalls even as fear sets him hopping backward), and its mouth opens to reveal rows of teeth.

The horror of those teeth is tempered, at least, by the fact that the monster seems to be struggling for its life. The gills on either side of its throat flap open and closed, and the beast's pointed nose thrashes through the air.

Gogi's hands clamp over his eyes. "Is it dead yet?"

"Bring the water back, Banu!" Rumi says. "This fish needs it to breathe! We're killing that poor thing!"

Startled, Banu retracts the boundary of their air bubble, so that the many-toothed monster is once again submerged. It thrashes its way into the deep.

The narrowing curtain of air also means the vertical trees return to dark shapes looming in the distance.

Rumi goes over the image seared in his mind, and all the other sensations that he was too surprised to process when they were first happening: the plip-plop of small sea creatures falling to the ground, the surprised fish and eels and crabs, caught halfway between their normal watery world and the companions' airy one.

They move forward and there—right by Rumi's feet!—is another stranded sea creature. This one is floppy and shiny, with many arms extending from its body and a pulsating sac in its middle. Two eyes blink up at Rumi while the body turns red. There are little cups all up and down the arms!

"Would you look at that, everyone—" Rumi says. But the creature has already used its many arms to crawl off into the watery deep.

"How amazing is all this?" Rumi asks his friends. "I wish I'd had a chance to try to talk to it!" The shadowwalkers stare back with widened eyes. Sky nods numbly.

"How's everyone doing?" Rumi asks.

"You know . . . a little . . . overwhelmed," Banu says.

Rumi nods. Apparently the intrigue of the new environment isn't enough to overcome his friends' feelings of intimidation at the novelty of it all. Good to know! There's always some new complication of the heart for Rumi to figure out.

What they really need is Lima here to take the lead,

to bring her cheer and excitement. But what they have is Rumi, and he's not exactly keeping morale up. Even normally irrepressible Gogi has his hands over his eyes.

Leader? Rumi? Stranger things have happened. Just a few days ago, he thought his friends would never trust him again if they knew the truth about his origins—and now it turns out they accept him anyway. Still, even if the trust and respect are there, he'll have to puzzle through how to do the actual leading part. Leaders are inspiring, right? They have lofty rhetoric and a call to action. Maybe he should give a rhyming speech and cry one dramatic tear at the end of it while screaming "for Caldera!" No, that doesn't seem like something he can manage.

Auriel slips off into the sea. That's strange. Rumi will have to close his speech with a stirring call instead to go investigate where Auriel has gone off to.

Rumi coughs and takes a long moment to collect himself when he sees his friends staring at him. He puffs out his chest and starts. "Since the dawn of time, the animals of the rainforest have wondered. Wondered about the future of their world, about its origins and limits, wondered about—"

"Run!" Gogi shrieks.

Rumi whirls to see a tentacle—bigger than the ones on the strange little blob that slithered away before, *much* bigger—whip into the bubble of air and thrash around. Gogi leaps away, his head breaking through the water membrane before he hurtles back to the ocean floor, spluttering and coughing. Sky hops away from the backhanding tentacle, nearly tumbling out of the bubble and into the sea. Rumi ducks into a piece of white bone. The tentacle strikes it, but the bone holds. He's safe— for now.

There are more of the terrifying tentacles. Two and then three of them whip through the open air, darting in and out of the ocean as they fish for the shadowwalkers. On the far side of the watery membrane, a big eye, wide as a cane toad, stares into the open air.

Banu, of course, can't move as quickly as the others. "Uh . . . oh," he says as he begins his stately retreat. At first the tentacles seem to be avoiding him—maybe the monster assumes he's an inanimate object. But then one strikes him by accident, and then it's wrapped around the sloth, once and twice and three times.

Rumi sends a blast of air at the tentacles, but his magical power seems particularly unsuited to fighting muscular wet tentacles.

Gogi, though, sends out a blast of fire as soon as he gets his feet and hands on the seafloor. It sizzles when it hits the tentacle, filling the air with steam and the smell of burning flesh. The next tentacle lashes out at

Gogi and, as soon as it contacts him, wraps around the monkey's body, pinning his tail against him. Gogi sends out a burst of flame from his skin, and the popping blast causes the arm to retreat. The capuchin rolls and goes right back on the offensive, popping small balls of fire at the tentacle gripping Banu. It slackens, and that only makes Gogi increase his attack, sending out pebbles of flame, one from each finger. *Pop pop pop pop!*

The tentacle leaves the air entirely. For a moment the giant eyeball is still there, lingering on the other side of the membrane—then it too disappears. Apparently the monster has decided there's easier quarry to be found elsewhere.

While Banu was being attacked, the perimeter of the air bubble came dangerously close. Now he lets out slack so that there's more air, enough space that the smell of burning monster and singed fur can dissipate.

"What just happened to us?" Gogi asks.

"I have no idea what that creature was," Rumi says.

"We don't have time to figure it out, either," Sky says. "Auriel left, and it clearly was for a reason. I think he was trying to get us to leave the area before the monster attacked. We should go catch up to him, as soon as possible."

Rumi looks in the direction Auriel went. A line of yellow light ribbons along the bottom of the sea. At least

Auriel won't be too hard to track. With the snake outside the bubble, the surroundings have turned dim. Another reason to catch up to Auriel quickly: it's bad enough to be on the bottom of the sea—Rumi would rather not be on the bottom of the sea and in the pitch-black to boot.

"Banu, can you go on or do you need to rest?" Rumi asks.

"I'm a napping expert . . . but to take a nap . . . here . . . while keeping up the bubble?" Banu says. "I'd prefer . . . to keep going . . . thanks."

"Okay," Sky says. "Let's move."

"No rest for the weary, as the saying goes," Rumi says.

"Especially no rest for the weary who are wandering around on the bottom of the sea," Gogi grumbles as he daintily steps around a spiny many-armed star sort of thing.

Knowing their sloth friend's limited reserves of energy, Rumi aims a jet of air at Banu's back, to give him help moving forward. "Ooh . . . thanks, buddy," Banu says. "You're . . . dislodging all sorts of . . . parasites . . . that have been bothering me . . . for many Veil drops."

Rumi hadn't noticed those. He uses his sticky tongue to pluck the parasites from the air as they fall.

Lice, yum. They've even got a nice salty aftertaste from the ocean water. It might have been too long since his last meal, come to think of it.

Auriel seems to know just how far he can go without leaving their bubble in the dark. He pauses in the undersea space, glowing in the depths like a click beetle, waiting for the companions to near before he inches farther out.

"Fascinating," Rumi says. "Auriel appears to be able to breathe water, like the fish do. I never noticed any gill flaps. I wonder if they were hidden along his throat. Or perhaps Auriel can hold his breath for long periods of time, like the boto, and he'll come back to us to breathe air eventually. The physiology of the snake is widely understudied, probably because of our bias against reptiles. Bias against amphibians—or anything without cuddly fur—is a thing too, but reptiles have it especially bad. Except for turtles, which for some reason everyone loves."

"You're doing that thing," Sky says.

"What thing?" Rumi says.

Sky doesn't even slow down as he walks along the skeletal plants at the bottom of the sea. "When you're worried, you start getting intellectual instead of talking about whatever it is you're feeling."

"Talking about whatever it is I'm *feeling*?" Rumi asks,

his voice chirping off at the end. He hadn't considered that he might be feeling something.

"Yep," Sky says. He raises the crest of feathers on top of his head and hops, what Rumi has come to recognize is the macaw version of a smile.

"Oh," Rumi says, thinking about it. "I suppose the feeling I have is worry. I guess I'm worried?"

"There you go," Sky says gently. "That wasn't so hard."

"Huh!" Rumi says, his face brightening as he clambers over a piece of kelp. "Saying the feeling out loud makes it go away a little bit!"

"Yes," Sky says. "That's how emotions work."

"How interesting," Rumi says. "It's not like you provided some insight to help me, it was expressing the feeling that helped. Has anyone studied this effect?"

"Here we go again," Sky says, shaking his head.

"Hey, this stuff stings," Gogi says, leaping away from one of the plants with the moving colorful tentacles. He stares at his hands, where lines of red welts have appeared, like he's been lashed. "The ocean is *painful*."

"We should move around these bright live rocks," Sky says. "Who knows what defenses they might have."

"We . . . can't move around them," Banu says. He turns left and right, and as Rumi follows the sloth's gaze, he realizes what his friend means—the bright live rocks extend high in either direction, making a wall.

"Auriel seems to have made it to the top fine," Gogi says, pointing to the highest point ahead, where the glowing yellow snake is serenely perched, facing them through a length of ocean water.

"He's also a magically resurrected Elemental of Light," Sky says dryly.

"Is it wrong that I'm sort of hoping that he attracts the attention of that tentacle monster, so it doesn't come back looking for *us* again?" Gogi asks, hands on his hips.

"If that's wrong, I don't want to be right," Sky says, nodding.

Gogi scratches his head.

Sky clucks impatiently. "What that phrase means is—"

"No more chitchat," Rumi says, hopping to Banu's back and holding on tight to the sloth's coarse fur. "I have a *plan!*"

"Ooh!" Gogi says, clapping his hands. "Rumi's plans are the *best.*"

"Sky, you go against Banu's belly. Gogi, you hug Banu, so that Sky's trapped in the middle. We don't want him falling away."

Sky looks between the parasite-ridden sloth and the soggy monkey. "Are you sure this is necessary?"

"Now, Sky," Rumi commands. Or as close as he

can get to commanding. It's unnerving to suddenly feel responsible for everyone.

Sky snaps to attention. "Okay, okay." He always was good at following orders. The macaw stands sideways, right in front of Banu, looking around nervously.

Gogi bounds over and hugs his two friends tight. "Aww. How snuggly!"

"What do I do?" Banu sputters.

"Nothing. Actually, keep up the sphere of air. That's, um, critically important. I figured that went without saying."

"Let's make it official that keeping up the air bubble goes without saying until we're back on the surface," Gogi says.

"Just hurry up. And it's really a hemisphere, not a sphere," Sky says, his voice muffled by mammal fur on either side.

"It is for *now*, you mean!" Rumi says. "Here we go!"

With that, secured on Banu's back, he faces the seafloor, opens his mouth, and emits a blast of air.

The companions hurtle up from the bottom and right into the ocean, the air popping as it becomes a perfect sphere around them.

Almost as soon as they've lifted off, they tilt toward the coral. Before Rumi can correct their course, Gogi's back rakes along its sharp surface. "Ow, ow, ow!"

"Sorry!" Rumi says, turning his head so the blast can correct their trajectory. Now they careen in the opposite direction, hurtling into the depths. At least there don't seem to be any obstacles this way, just the dark, cold water around them. Rumi reverses the blast, and they go jetting off again.

"Does anyone have a sense of where we are?" he asks, turning this way and that, peering into the inky darkness. They begin to descend while he tries to get his bearings.

"Auriel is . . . right in front of me," Banu says. Rumi pivots to see the glowing yellow line of the snake coursing toward them through the depths. He holds still in the water, waiting for them to follow.

"On it!" Rumi says. By now he's gotten a better sense of how his blasts interact with the water, and sets a smoother course this time around. The water parts around them, rippling in the scant light coming from distant Auriel. As they fly through the seawater, for the most part Rumi's attention is focused on controlling his stream of air. But when they pass close to one of the vertical trees, he can't help but give it a close look.

The edge of the structure is covered in seaweed and the bright bony creatures, but where the coverings part, Rumi can see the glint of the same hard, shiny substance that surrounded the magical lens. If it's the same material as the artifact, then it's a two-leg creation, something that has been lost since they went extinct. In the carvings, the two-legs didn't appear to be underwater, and Rumi can only assume that they're seeing them in a different environment than when they were built. What happened, then? Why are they submerged now?

An eel slithers out of one seaweed-clogged rectangular opening in the structure, and into another. It's not quite like the freshwater eels Rumi has met; this one has a long frill along its back, speckled skin, and—gulp—big teeth. Unlike the tentacled monster from before, this creature is more scared than aggressive. It secrets itself away.

They fly their spherical wall-less ship past more of the vertical trees. Mounds fill the paths between the structures, covered in the same brightly colored lifeforms, waving their fans and tentacles in the seawater. Giant humped creatures, just as he saw back in the Cave of Riddles.

"It's those . . . strange giant animals with circles for legs that were journeying into the volcano," Rumi says to Sky between breaths.

"Yes!" Sky says. "That means we're going the right way."

They continue to float through the eerie two-leg

ruins. The round-legged beasts must be long dead, because they've been covered by sea growth. If only Rumi had time to investigate more, to clear away some of the debris and see these extinct rounded animals up close . . . ah well, the fate of all Caldera takes precedence, he knows that. But if they manage to stop the volcano, then maybe Rumi can return with Banu, do some real research into the rainforest's past.

Some of the vertical trees—which the two-legs probably built somehow, Rumi's realizing—have fallen over, tumbled one into the next. Auriel leads them across an encrusted span that crests a sea ravine, the line of stopped round-footed beasts leading along it into the undersea side of the rainforest mountain. Is the span the skeleton of some great beast, longer than the tallest ironwood tree? Maybe the rounded creatures were parasites that felled the giant creature. Or maybe they were all slain at the same time, when the two-legs died, and their vertical trees succumbed to the sea. Or maybe they're not animals at all, none of them.

Auriel swims the open water, fearlessly passing through the mysterious depths. The four shadowwalkers stay huddled close, Sky making little caws of protest as Gogi and Banu smoosh him between them.

As they pass over the elegant length of rubble (which

Rumi decides is not a skeleton after all, but something the two-legs probably built; its bottom is too flat to be organic), Auriel slows and stops in the open water.

"Do I bring us right up to him?" Rumi asks between breaths.

"I'd say so. Auriel is our only guide point," Sky wheezes. "Who's squishing my left wing?"

"Oh, sorry!" Banu says, adjusting his shoulder so that Sky is freed. Then he paces forward. The bubble continues toward Auriel, the yellow squiggle of him growing until—*plop!*—he's inside the bubble. He falls right through, until Gogi grabs him by the tail. The boa constrictor entwines around the trio.

"Good work, Gogi," Rumi says.

"Grabbing a snake by the tail goes against every monkey instinct I have," Gogi says.

Rumi knows the feeling. As Auriel wraps around them, it comes to him how easily the snake could squeeze and kill them all. But he saved them from the Ant Queen, and has been useful on this anti-volcano journey so far. Still, there are times when the creep factor of their one-time adversary gets a little too high.

"I think he's gotten bigger . . . even just down here in the sea," Banu says.

He's right. Auriel rings them all in glowing yellow

coils. He's as big as he ever was before his resurrection.

"Auriel, buddy," Gogi says. "This is tight enough, thanks."

Auriel obliges, loosening his coils. While the friends hover in the sea, Rumi blasts just enough air out to keep them level, finessing their direction. Auriel brings his head toward the far side of the span and flicks his tongue in one specific direction. It's clear what he's doing: in his own snake way, he's pointing.

At what, though? The water gets dark so quickly. Rumi squints into the watery distance, trying to make out where Auriel's directing their attention.

"Here's an idea," Gogi says. "Banu, if I send out an arrow of fire, can you make the water part for it?"

"Hmm," Banu says. "Let me see."

"Give it just a couple of attempts, and then we'll have to figure out something else," Rumi says. "I'm starting to get exhausted from all this wind blowing."

"Three, two . . . one!" Gogi says, releasing a bolt of flame. Just as he promised, Banu parts the water for it—but a good dozen frog-lengths too low.

"Sorry, sorry," Banu says. "Try another."

Gogi counts down again, and releases another bolt of flame. This time Banu parts the water in just the right spot, making an arcing tunnel through the dark. It illuminates the seafloor—fish and kelp and bright bony outcroppings—and the hulking remnants of the lost two-leg world. As it continues, though, it heads toward the side of the undersea mountain that's the base of Caldera, and illuminates something else entirely.

The motionless line of rounded beasts heads into an archway that passes into the earth. There's something unutterably beautiful about it to Rumi. The archway is a perfect parabola, with a mathematical pureness that Rumi has seen only in spiderwebs and the motion of projectiles like Gogi's flame bolt.

"I think the two-legs constructed that entrance through their magic," Rumi breathes.

"Do you have enough strength to propel us over there, buddy?" Gogi asks.

Rumi nods. At least he thinks he does.

He takes in a deep breath and slowly releases it behind the group, propelling them through the cold darkness. Gogi keeps up a stream of directions: "Up a little, now left a little, no, *your* right so we *go* left, that's it, that's good, Banu, I'm sending out another bolt, wonderful, great, thanks, okay, Rumi, let's go higher, perfect, one more burst and then turn around."

Rumi is relieved when he gets Gogi's last direction, letting out a final gust before pivoting. The water slows them, the bubble descending as gravity takes over. Rumi worries that he misunderstood Gogi's instructions, that they're just going to sink to the bottom of the sea. But as they float downward, they come to rest on a flat surface. It's covered in sand that's hiding some flat fish that swim away, startled, as the sphere of air lands on them.

They're inside the two-legs' structure.

The tunnelway beckons before them.

**16**

"I NEED . . . JUST a few minutes," Banu says, before collapsing on the tunnel floor. His snores fill the air. Rumi wouldn't have thought that a bubble could have an echo, but here it is. He also wouldn't have thought any creature could take a nap under the ocean, but here's that, too.

"How long do we give him?" Gogi asks, nudging the comatose sloth.

"There's no pushing a sloth past its limits," Rumi says. "Let's let him have his power nap."

"He did this once before, keeping his water power up while sleeping," Gogi says admiringly. "I wish I could manage that."

"I think it's in all of our best interests that your fire power does *not* stay active while you're asleep," Sky notes.

"Yeah, I get some vivid dreams," Gogi says. "Say, I wonder if the Veil has dropped yet over the land. This is the first time I haven't known what's going on with the sun. It dictates so much of our lives up there."

Rumi nods, rubbing his froggy fingers over his body for warmth. "Yes. Maybe it shouldn't. Dictate so much of our lives, that is."

"Here you go, buddy, here's some heat," Gogi says as he crouches and creates a little fire on the kelp-strewn floor of the tunnel. The moisture beneath it sizzles and evaporates. Then there's just the crackling of crisping seaweed.

"Thanks," Rumi says, huddling near the flames and holding his hands out. "That helps. Being cold-blooded is a pain sometimes."

Gogi's meager fire makes the tunnel on the far side even darker. What awaits them down its length? Rumi can't help but shudder at the thought of it.

Sky keeps a careful distance from the fire, like any creature covered in feathers should, but Rumi does notice the macaw's beak parting in relief as he holds out his wings, catching some of the radiant heat.

Auriel doesn't seem pleased by the group's break. He

slithers around the perimeter of their air bubble, dipping in and out of the surrounding water. His pacing casts rippling yellows through the membrane.

"I could stare at that shifting yellow light forever," Gogi says, leaning back on the ground with his hands behind his head. "It's so mesmerizing."

"It also lights us up for any enemies to see," Sky says.

Gogi sits straight, bites his fingernails. Rumi knows the monkey well enough by now to see the exact thought passing behind his friend's eyes: *Uh-oh, tentacles, uh-oh.* True to form, Gogi looks around for something to eat to cut his anxiety. His eyes light on an odd star-shaped organism. Before Rumi can say, "I don't think you should," Gogi's brought it to his mouth and taken a bite.

"Phugh!" Gogi says, spitting out a rubbery hunk of the animal. The remaining four arms writhe in his hand. He tosses the star creature into the wall of ocean. "Oh my gosh, you're alive, I'm so sorry, I thought you were a plant! Ack!"

"You know, even if that had been a plant, it technically would have been alive," Rumi says. "It just wouldn't have been an *animal.*"

"Ah," Gogi says as he frantically rubs his fingers over his tongue. "Whatever it was, I'm definitely not glad that I took a bite out of it. Blech."

Rumi's body shakes, and at first he assumes his shivering has returned. Then he sees Sky looking about, head tilted. It's the ground itself that's trembling. "What is that?" Gogi asks.

"Isn't it obvious?" Sky asks. "We're nearing the volcano's interior, and it's about to erupt. Of course there's bound to be seismic activity."

"Sheesh, I was just asking," Gogi says.

The rumbling stops, but as it does, the water ripples strangely. "Well, would you look at—" Rumi starts to say. Before he can finish, the edge of the bubble pushes unexpectedly, shoving them toward the tunnel entrance. They're bowled over by the surprise of it more than anything else, and are just getting back to their claws and feet when the water pushes again, the force of it this time jetting them right out of the tunnel.

The sphere of air holds for a moment and then it disintegrates, frittering away into a million tiny bubbles. Rumi is suddenly floating in the freezing darkness, unable to hear or see his friends, saltwater stinging his skin all over, cold sapping the life force out of him, his tender eardrums aching with pressure. He flails through the seawater, the pain sharp now, like thorns in his flesh. Rumi's thoughts scatter. He looks for light in the dark as his eyes sear with the salt.

Even in his panic, Rumi's thoughts go to his mammal

friends—if they've started gulping in seawater, they're done for.

There—a new sphere of light, hanging in the undersea like a glowing mushroom. Rumi swims toward it, but he can't make any headway against the currents coming out of the tunnel. He's pushed farther and farther away from light and safety . . . until he remembers his air power.

Rumi turns away from the direction of the blast, and emits the most powerful stream of air that he can. It sends him hurtling blind through the sea, mouth open in a silent scream as he strengthens his jet. He can only hope that he calibrated his bearing well enough, that he's not a few degrees off and hurtling into the unknown deep.

Then, with a pop and a sputter, he's in open air again. Rumi reaches out an arm to grab Banu's fur, misses, then shoots his sticky tongue out on reflex. It contacts Banu's ear, and Rumi uses it to lasso himself to his friend. Sky's there too, held tight in Banu's arms. But where is Gogi?

The yellow light dims, and before Rumi can tell where Auriel has gone, the boa constrictor is back, holding a sorry soggy form tight in his rear coils. Auriel releases Gogi onto the tunnel floor, where the monkey lies on his side, horribly and terribly still.

"He's not . . . he's not breathing!" Banu says.

Sky turns his head so he can listen to Gogi's lips, then shakes his head.

Rumi's skin, still stinging from the seawater, goes clammy instead. No—it can't be. He hops to his friend, tugs on Gogi's fingers. "Get up, Gogi! Get up!"

He's motionless.

Tears stream from Rumi's eyes. "No. No!"

"Rumi, what do we do?" Sky caws.

"No, Gogi!" Rumi wails.

"Rumi, perhaps your magic . . . ?"

Rumi's snuffles stop. "My magic?"

"So Gogi can breathe?"

"Oh my gosh, oh my gosh," Rumi says, then hops to Gogi's chin. "Sky, could you help?"

Sky doesn't need any more direction. The macaw uses his agile claws to part Gogi's mouth. Rumi leans forward and sends a gentle gust, then a stronger one. Gogi's ribs rise and fall with the force of it.

But he's still motionless.

Rumi tries again.

The monkey sputters and turns onto his side. He coughs up great mouthfuls of seawater, and if Rumi's not incorrect, his star-creature lunch. Gogi rolls over onto his back again. "Wow. What just happened to me?" he asks.

"Gogi!" Rumi says. "You're okay!"

"Let's make sure that nothing like that ever happens again," Gogi rasps. "That was horrible."

Sky surprises Rumi by wrapping his wings around Gogi. "I'm glad you're okay."

"Thanks to Rumi," Gogi gasps.

"It was Auriel that saved you, really," Rumi says. "He went to fetch you."

Auriel stares at them, expressionless, then arrows out of Banu's air bubble and farther into the tunnel.

"Thank you!" Gogi calls after him.

"That was the absolute . . . worst," Banu says, shaking his shaggy head. "I was having . . . the most wonderful dream . . . and then suddenly . . . we were all drowning."

"And it could happen again at any moment, when the volcano rumbles next," Sky caws. "So let's get following Auriel, quickly. No more resting."

"Okay, okay," Banu says, starting his slow progress along the tunnel floor. "You don't have . . . to ask me twice."

"Maybe next time we sense a rumble, you can put some extra water pressure up against it," Rumi suggests as he hops to a position on top of Gogi's head, holding on to the tufts of fur over his eyes. "That way, hopefully our air bubble won't break."

"I think I can . . . do that," Banu says. "I wasn't even . . . awake last time . . . so it wasn't a fair chance."

Auriel threads himself along the boundary of their air bubble, illuminating the entire membrane in yellow. Banu crawls forward, the friends making a protective circle around him. As they progress, Rumi's eyes dart around the front of the open space, alert to any more rumbles from the volcano.

*Plop plop plop.*

Rumi cringes, readying his wind magic for whatever enemy has come upon them. But there's no ruckus, no rush of water or sizzle of magic. Instead, he opens his eyes to see three fish on the ground, gasping, eyes wide.

"Oh, poor little guys," Gogi says. "We surprised them." He picks the fish up one by one, and tosses them through the membrane behind them.

As the group treks forward, they continue to surprise sea creatures that drop onto the tunnel floor. Once they come across a whole school of small orange fish, too many for Gogi to rescue. Instead Banu speeds up, letting the water pick the fish back up on the far side before too much time has gone by.

The tunnel stays remarkably level, passing right into the mountain. There's a stream of the rounded still creatures along it—or rather, two streams. They're closer to them than ever before, now; if he dared to, Rumi could reach out and touch one. He examines them as they pass, trying to figure out their mystery, and realizes that the shapes are a little more elongated on one side, depending on which of the two streams the creature is in. Almost like they're . . .

"They were moving in different directions!" Rumi exclaims.

"What?" Sky asks, startled.

"These big rounded beasts. Before they died, they were traveling in an orderly way, one after the other, in two different lines. I've never seen anything like it."

"Except for ants," Sky says, leaning close to one of the rounded creatures and bravely scraping his beak all along its length. "Ants do that."

"That's true!" Rumi says. "Maybe the two-legs were relatives of ants."

"They both appear to have highly structured, cooperative societies," Sky says. "Unlike any other animals in Caldera." The macaw hops on top of one of the seaweed-covered giant beasts, works his beak into the growth covering it.

"What are you doing?" Rumi asks, garnering up enough courage to hop to Sky's side so as to get a better view.

"It's as I thought," Sky says between scrapings. "These rounded creatures are made of different materials. Mostly they're made of something hard and smooth, like rock, and the four circular things connecting the creatures to the ground are soft and bouncy, whereas these panels, like the one I'm scraping now, are . . . yes! Take a look."

Gogi joins them as Sky steps back, cawing triumphantly. "What is it?"

Rumi hops forward, wipes a hand over the surface Sky just cleared with his beak. "Oh wow, it's as clear as the lens. And on the other side . . . Gogi, could you give us a little firelight?"

"Of course," Gogi says, creating a ball of flame that hovers above his palm. "Hey, Banu," he calls down, "pause for a minute here, okay?"

Banu's exhausted voice wafts up. "Not . . . a problem."

The three friends lean into the surface. Inside the rounded shape are lumpy things, hard to make out, and a circular device right in front. Attached are two bony appendages, leading to . . .

"A skeleton!" Rumi exclaims.

"Ew, gross," Gogi says.

"No, it's fascinating," Rumi says. "Look, the same bones you see in frog hands and feet, only longer, and the skull is similar, though a different overall shape, of course. But this creature is no longer alive."

"Enough talk," Gogi says worriedly. "Let's not delay anymore, okay?"

"It's all we have left of them, but it's more than we've ever seen of them before, in the flesh," Sky continues. "Not that there's any actual flesh to speak of, but you catch my meaning."

"It's all we have left of *who*?" Gogi asks, scratching his head.

"The two-legs."

**17**

"Wow," Gogi says, bowing close to the clear stone panel. "We're seeing history right in front of us. Poor two-legs, eaten by these rounded creatures that moved single file like ants."

Sky nods sadly. "I guess the rounded creatures digested everything but the skeletons."

Rumi's face crinkles. "Why would the two-legs be in this regular position, instead of the bones all jumbled up? We've all dissected owl pellets to see what's inside, right? The bones are all a mess."

"I'd like to note for the official record that I have never dissected an owl pellet," Gogi says. "Nor do I particularly want to."

"I almost think that these two-legs decided to go inside the rounded beasts," Rumi says. "Like they thought they wouldn't get digested, or something."

"Sure, okay, weird but okay. Above my brain power to figure out," Gogi says.

"Mine too," Sky caws.

Rumi peers deeper into the rounded beast, soaking in all the details he can. Lengths of something that looks like woven vine fasten the two-legs into their position. Like they were trapped there.

"We should get moving," Sky says. "Before the volcano rumbles again."

"I'm getting hungry, too," Gogi says, holding his belly, "and I don't plan on trying out any new seafood. Blech."

As if on cue, another rumble comes from the tunnel ahead. Rumi prepares to mount a rescue, but this time Banu is ready. The membrane trembles, but the bubble of air holds fast. Sky and Gogi clamber to the tunnel floor, Gogi holding up his hand so Rumi can use it to hop down more easily.

His mind running over and over the puzzle of the extinct two-leg civilization, Rumi loses track of time as they pass forward. The line of rounded beasts is seemingly endless.

For a while, Gogi keeps up a firelight to warm them,

but eventually the monkey's fur is matted with sweat, dripping even from the tip of his tail. Rumi taps him on the shoulder. "I think the temperature is rising," Rumi says. "You can probably drop the fire."

Gogi startles, then pats his own body. The fire disappears. "You're right. I guess I'm a little distracted."

"Are you saying that heading right into the heart of a volcano, with all the weight of our rainforest over our heads, is worrying you?" Sky asks dryly.

"Yes," Gogi says. "Was that not clear?"

"No, no, it was, I was joking," Sky sputters. He caws a sigh. "Maybe I should just go back to being quiet."

"It was a good joke, buddy, my bad, keep 'em coming," Gogi says, patting Sky awkwardly on the head.

They continue along, the only sounds the plop of surprised fish passing into the bubble and the rhythmic rush and flow of the waves around them. Rumi falls into a reverie, his thoughts back on his many developing theories about the meaning of the tunnel, the rounded beasts, and the two-leg skeletons inside them.

The reverie is broken by a booming voice ahead. "Who disturbs my slumber?"

The companions go still. "Please tell me that was one of you guys," Gogi whispers.

"Come forward," the voice says. "I would like to

see that yellow light closer. And it has been a very long time since I have eaten."

"That sounds like a good argument . . . for *not* getting any closer," Banu says.

Auriel has other ideas, though. The glowing snake slithers toward the booming voice, leaving the air bubble behind.

"Auriel!" Rumi hisses. But the snake is already gone.

"Well, that's not good," Sky says.

"Is the voice we heard . . . one of the two-legs?" Banu asks.

"Given their mass, I don't think any of the two-legs could make a sound like that," Rumi says. "Besides, I think they really are all extinct. I'd be surprised if we found one now."

There's a low rhythmic rumbling sound that comes with undulations of the membrane. It takes Rumi a few moments to recognize it as laughter. "I am no two-leg. Come closer, and you will see what I am."

"Again, going to officially suggest we don't do what the scary booming voice says," Gogi whispers.

"I don't think we have a choice," Sky says. "The only way forward is into the mountain."

They look down along the stream of stilled curved beasts, deep into the tunnel, farther from air and light. Farther from safety.

Auriel has already started down the passage, is a good dozen snake-lengths ahead. "If we want Auriel with us when we face whoever's voice that is, we'd better get moving," Rumi says.

"Gulp," Gogi says.

Banu starts forward, Rumi on his head, Gogi on one flank, Sky on the other. Another roar from the mountain, another surge against the air bubble, Banu fighting back again. Together, the companions continue.

The rounded beasts stop, and the ground beneath them becomes rougher, casting upward in chaotic formations. Gogi scouts ahead, finding the best route for slower-moving Banu to navigate the obstacles. The tunnel's ceiling rises so it's no longer within the air bubble; Rumi has no idea whether it's vaulting high above, or right over their heads.

As the shadowwalkers pass forward, Rumi notices that the path into the mountain has become almost featureless—there's little growing on the floor of the tunnel. Like they're too far from the open ocean for anything to survive.

Except for one thing, at least.

Ahead is Auriel's yellow glow.

Beyond it are two giant green orbs.

Eyes.

T HE GREEN ORBS blink once, twice. A mouth opens, and the reflected light from Auriel plays over long pointed teeth. "You have come to your end," the mouth says.

"What are you?" Gogi calls out, fear making his voice break.

"I am the largest, I am the withdrawn, I am the core of Caldera."

Gogi looks at his friends, as if to see if any of them has understood, but they just blink back, confused. Gogi clears his throat. "Does a withdrawn eat monkeys?"

Auriel coils himself up, facing the jaw and the green

eyes. Almost like he's hoping to protect the group from the giant stranger.

Heart racing, Rumi takes a hop forward. He can see more of the creature now. It's a fish, and easily the biggest one Rumi has ever seen. "I have lived many eons down here, to grow to this size," it says. "I was once known as a grouper, but I no longer see any of my kind. If any came to visit me now, I would eat them."

It makes a raspy, groaning laugh, sending clouds of debris up from the tunnel floor. Sky looks at Rumi, feathers pricked: *What is this fish's deal?*

Rumi hops forward again, so he's on top of Auriel's coils. "We need to get past you, because this tunnel heads to the volcano under Caldera, and we need to plug the volcano," he says. "That will save our rainforest. It will save you."

The fish blinks heavily. "You lie. Plugging the volcano would mean collapsing the tunnel. Collapsing the tunnel would mean killing me."

"It would not have to," Sky caws. "You could leave first."

"Oh, I could leave, could I?" the grouper says. "Is it that simple?"

"Yes, actually," Sky says.

"I chose to leave the world of other fish long ago,"

the grouper says. "This is my seclusion. I will not leave this tunnel."

Banu crawls forward. "We have to pass. Time is running out."

"What will prevent me from eating you?" the grouper asks.

"Nothing," Banu says. "We will still try, though."

As Banu crawls past Auriel, the boa constrictor stretches out, so he's always at the front of the line as they near the giant fish. It opens its mouth, again displaying long, sharp teeth. "You might think your actions are brave. I think they are foolish."

Banu takes another step forward. The grouper lunges toward him, and as it does, Auriel, with instant reflexes, opens his mouth and strikes. His teeth had been removed by bullying snakes when he was young, and he didn't gain them back in resurrected form, but of course the grouper doesn't know that. The fish hesitates, and it's just long enough for Rumi to send out a blast of air that nudges the grouper farther back in the tunnel, enough that its jaws don't contact Banu.

"You have magic," the fish says, its booming voice sending gusting waves against the bubble's membrane. "There's a chance you could actually succeed in your task."

"Of course we'll succeed!" Gogi says.

"Your success is meaningless to me," the grouper says. "Nothing has meaning except my solitary life, and I will not let you take that away." It lunges at Banu again, mouth wide as its mass surges through the water.

Gogi's the first to react this time, readying the same flame arrows that he used to scout out the terrain when they were approaching the tunnel. He creates one in each palm and shoots them out, sizzling as they hit the far side of the bubble. Just as the grouper's face emerges into the air, they pass through the membrane, hitting the fish on the jaw. The arrows fizzle too soon to do much damage, but once again the grouper goes on the retreat.

"Why are you doing this?" it asks. "Why do you insist on resisting me?"

"We need to pass!" Rumi says. "Please, it's very important."

"You mean to destroy my home," the grouper says. "Is that *not* important to you?"

Gogi wrings his hands. "We're in a bit of a moral bind, aren't we?"

"No, we're not," Sky says hotly. "One grouper's life against the welfare of all Caldera? There's no choice there."

"I can see both your points," Rumi says. "I certainly

don't want to be a murderer, but the good of our entire land seems much more important than one fish's life. There's also an additional concern to weigh, of course: we run the risk of being *eaten* by the grouper before we can get past it."

"Yes, you do run that risk," the grouper booms. "And I have very good hearing, just so you know. I can actually feel the vibrations of your voices along the pores of my lateral line. I sense sounds just like I do the currents of my prey's movements."

Rumi takes a deep breath. This is not an intellectual task, but a test of emotional logic. He hopes he's up to it.

He hops forward. One jump. Two, then three. He's nearly within striking range of the grouper's jaws. There, now he actually is. He takes another hop. He's past Auriel's coils. The giant fish wouldn't even need to bite him—it could just inhale Rumi through a nostril. It rises above him like a mountain.

"I had no idea about your lateral line," Rumi says. "I'm afraid my fish knowledge is very slim, and I hope that someday, once this is all over, we might be able to sit down—or swim down?—together, and you can tell me all about what it's like to be a fish. I was once a tadpole, but that's a quite different experience, I imagine."

"Rumi . . ." Sky says warningly.

"Right, right," Rumi says, clapping his froggy fingers

together. "I'm learning all about my comfort zones. Let me cut to the chase. It's quite clear to all of us here that you could eat us in one gulp, if you chose to. Maybe you *will* choose to. But I hope you will hear me out first. We've told you that we need to get past you and through the tunnel to plug the volcano that's going to blow up and destroy the rainforest. I thought that would matter to you, but it seems it doesn't. So let me try a different tack. Ahem."

Rumi takes a long breath, and looks back at his friends, who are watching him with an awkward sort of worry on their faces. Rumi returns to face the enormous grouper. "My friends think I'm crazy right now. Anyway, I think you should know that I had a rough start, as a tadpole, and as a young frog, and I made some mistakes that I deeply regret. I also . . . well, I guess I'm a little unusual in the amount that I think about things, and it makes it hard for me, um . . . for me to relate to the other animals sometimes. It took a while for me to become friends with this crew behind me."

The grouper's eyes wander over the bedraggled companions, then go almost cross-eyed as it returns its attention to Rumi. "Go on," it says.

"All that's to say that I can understand why you would become a hermit and hide yourself away in this tunnel. The world can be a harsh place, and it can seem easier just to withdraw, because of all the emotional confusion. I don't know what you've been through, and I can't pretend to understand it, not being . . . um, a sea creature myself. But I'll tell you this: if you'd like, after this is all done, I'd like to come back with the help of my friend Banu here, and I'd like to get to know you better. I want to hear your story. I want to tell you our story. We've all been living alongside one another for eons, but the land and air creatures don't know the first thing about the ones who live in the sea. That seems like a shame."

The grouper opens its jaws even wider, Auriel's glow reflecting on the back of its massive throat. Then it closes them. "It does seem like a shame, when you put it that way."

The force of the grouper's booming voice is enough to bowl Rumi out of the air bubble. He swims back in and plops to his hands and feet, nodding vigorously while Gogi rubs him warm. "I promise you this, on my amphibian honor, that I will come find you again when I can."

The grouper wriggles its spiny dorsal fin. "I would like that. You may pass."

Rumi looks at his friends, raising his little frog arms in a cheer.

The shadowwalkers don't look excited. They look . . . suspicious. Gogi raises an eyebrow, a flame arrow already

249

in place above his palm. Sky cocks his head, his beak open in a silent caw. Banu—well, actually Banu looks ready for a nap.

"Come on, we have to trust the grouper," Rumi says, taking another hop forward.

The grouper holds there, motionless, watching the frog as he approaches. Gogi, Banu, and Sky slowly make their way behind. Auriel passes alongside, pausing every length or so to taste the air, as if to smell the grouper's intentions.

As he gets ever closer to the giant fish, Rumi's heart starts to race, and he can feel toxins tingling on his back. "Watch out, guys, I'm envenomating," he warns. But he keeps moving forward, all the same.

As they get even nearer, Gogi balks, but then, watching Rumi hop forward, the monkey seems to find the courage to continue. They're all within range of the jaws now. The fish opens and closes its mouth, watching them silently.

The grouper is only slightly smaller than the width of the tunnel. Once they get near enough, of course, Banu's air bubble will contain the fish, too. "You might not be able to breathe through your gills for a moment," Rumi warns. "Once we're past, though, the water will return."

"This will be a new experience," the grouper says,

and then its eyes widen in surprise as the air bubble hits it. The fish splashes to the floor, flips its fins helplessly, and in the process rolls onto its side, nearly on top of the companions.

"Whoa, whoa, whoa," Gogi says, scrambling up the side of the tunnel. But the grouper manages to stop itself before it crushes them all. The shadowwalkers pass along its green-black scales, no one daring to make any loud noises or otherwise startle the giant fish.

Finally they come to the tail, and they can hear a rushing sound behind them as the grouper's gills take in water. "Phew," the grouper burbles.

"Thank you!" Rumi calls back. "You might want to wait out in the open ocean for a while, in case we manage to plug the volcano. And I meant what I said—I'll come find you after this is all done."

"If we're alive," Sky adds.

"Right," Rumi says, gulping. "If we're alive."

"At least your lives aren't at risk from me anymore," the grouper says.

"Thanks," Rumi calls back.

"Doesn't feel like we should have to thank someone for not inhaling us," Gogi says under his breath.

"Shh," Sky says, with something like a giggle in his voice. It's the macaw version of a giggle, a sort of sprightly hoot.

Rumi takes a long last look at the grouper. Its massive tail barely moves as it hovers in the stagnant tunnel water; it doesn't seem to be trying to escape after all. Will they wind up entombing it, if they collapse the mountain? Rumi's journey started out with innocents dying. Will that happen all over again?

Rumi gets lost in his concerns as he rides forward on Gogi's head. Is suffering necessary, for any creatures at all to live? It's quite a question. This will take a lot of puzzling through.

The transition has been so gradual that Rumi almost misses that the tunnel isn't really a tunnel anymore. It's become a set of underwater caves. Banu leads them through a craggy cavern, the ground chill from the seawater and sharp from the pointy little armored creatures that live on it.

Three pathways lead from the bottom of the cavern, far narrower than the tunnel with the rounded beasts. It feels a little like they're back in the Cave of Riddles. Gogi leans into one tunnel, hands visoring his eyes as he squints. "Seems barely wide enough for Banu and me. I don't love the idea of going down there, I have to say. Give me the tallest tree you can imagine, and I'm good. Tight underground quarters, no thanks."

Rumi glances at Sky. "We navigated a cave system once before, back when we were searching for the lens.

Let us give this a shot. We'll scout out, and report back."

"If you're feeling that brave, be my guest," Gogi says.

Rumi hops between the three gaping passages, none more appealing than the others. "The question now is which one, I guess."

"Hmm," Sky says, peering into each one with his wide pitch-black eyes. "I'd say that this one on the left is the most—wow, would you look at that?"

Auriel had been motionless, staring at the companions as if waiting for them to notice him. Now he's gone into motion, slithering into the middle passage.

"I guess we have our choice?" Sky says.

"So it would seem," Rumi says, hopping after Auriel. "I'll follow first and make sure that the way isn't too narrow for any of you."

"I'll be right behind you . . . with the air bubble," Banu says.

"Yes, right, thanks," Rumi says. He slaps his palms, plucks up his courage, and then hops into the tunnel, keeping his focus on the yellow light blazing before him.

The glow of Auriel's tail highlights shiny stretches in the rock, sharp outcroppings that Rumi's able to avoid. If he were as big as his friends, though . . . "Watch your heads," he calls back to the others. "There are plenty of ways to cut yourselves along here."

The ground slopes. With fingers as sticky as Rumi's,

it's easy to keep his footing, but he's not sure how his friends will get by. It's hard to imagine Sky's claws, especially, gaining any purchase along the smooth black stone of the tunnel. "Hold on, guys!" Rumi calls up. "It's getting slippery along here."

"Thanks for the warning, buddy," comes Gogi's voice from up above, over the sound of Sky's clattering claws. "You're right about these outcroppings, by the way. Ouch!"

Rumi taps his fingers on the stone. It's getting more slippery and it's also getting . . . hotter?

Auriel never flags as he slithers along the smooth rock floor. Rumi falls farther and farther behind as he hops along. All the facts and figures in the world won't help him pick the right course here, but he can trust his heart instead and choose to follow Auriel, and let the snake's intuition guide the day. Maybe something about his resurrection as an Elemental of Light has given Auriel an intuitive connection to the earth itself. Stranger things have happened.

"Hold up, Auriel," Rumi calls. "I'm right behind you, but I won't be for long if you go *too* fast—oh no!" Auriel has sped up more and more, until he's shooting into an open shaft in the stone, free-falling down a chasm. Rumi sees it happen, but all his scrambling doesn't slow him enough. He's tumbling free, until he splooshes through Banu's membrane into deep, dark ocean water.

He chooses a direction at random and swims. The moment he has his wits about him, he looks for Auriel's yellow glow. He spies it far below, and heads toward it. Auriel's swimming too, not wasting any time waiting for Rumi to catch up. The little frog can keep the glow in sight, but only when he strokes as fast as he can.

He hopes his friends heeded his warning to wait—if they followed down this chasm without Banu, they'd be doomed. None of them can survive as long underwater as he can. It's not like Rumi can spend *too* long underwater, now that he's past his tadpole phase, but he can make it a few hours without breathing air. Normally he can breathe through his skin, but down here—he can't feel the usual ripples of fresh oxygen, and there's the sting of the salt. He needs to get back to air, or at least freshwater, as soon as he can.

Auriel's glow leads him farther and farther through the depths of the watery cave, until the yellow light pauses, increasing in intensity as Rumi approaches it— Auriel must have been stopped by something. Rumi catches up to him, clutching the scales at the boa constrictor's side as he works his way along his long body. Once he's on top of Auriel's head, Rumi can see what's caught his attention.

At the bottom of a chasm, great swirls of glowing red liquid bloom from the earth. Where they strike the water, the swirls turn black. As more and more of the red magma spews out, its level rises, passing higher and higher up the walls of the chasm.

The water's so hot here. Rumi's eyes sting, and his skin feels like it's crawling and crinkling. All the same, he can't look away. This is the origin of it all. This is the source of the looming destruction of Caldera, the magma that was once held at bay by the magic of the two-legs, that has been freed through the plotting of the now-dead Ant Queen.

He's witnessing the coming of the end of the world.

NOTHING RUMI'S SEEN before could compare to this. The heat and the chill, the darkness and the light, all combining into a roiling mass . . . it's something that should exist in some other time, in some other world, but it is right in front of him. Rumi's undone, his mind whirring as he watches.

Auriel isn't undone, though. He looks down placidly, then looks back at Rumi. He really *sees* Rumi, and the tree frog realizes it's for the first time. Until this moment, Auriel has treated the shadowwalkers like inanimate objects, like moving trees or grasses. But now the enormous yellow snake seems to be trying to communicate something.

"What do you need me to do?" Rumi asks. Even at a whisper, his words boom in the water.

Auriel shakes his head. *Nothing.* Then he looks down toward the roiling mass of magma and dark water. He looks back at Rumi.

"What are you thinking?" Rumi asks. His skin is already crawling from the heat and salt, but also, now, from an extra source of tension: *What is Auriel planning?*

Auriel flicks his tongue up in the direction they came. *Go back.*

He wants Rumi to leave?

Rumi shakes his head. Retreat before they've accomplished their goal? No way. His lungs feel empty, like his front ribs are pulling against his backbone, but he's got some time left down here yet before he starts really suffocating.

Auriel turns his attention to the steamy cauldron down below. He flicks his tongue out, tasting the hot salty water, laced with ash and bits of rock, so far below the surface of Caldera.

Then Auriel moves.

His thick, glowing body ripples through the water as it descends toward the surging magma and water.

"Auriel!" Rumi calls. But there's no chance Auriel

could hear him over the boiling turmoil below. Rumi can only watch as the bright yellow beams cast shadows over the undersea cavern, lighting mysterious glints of this innermost cavity beneath their rainforest home. Auriel's powerful coils propel him down, down, until he's nearly at the source of the magma itself, at the red-and-black boil that is the center of the plumes of ashy water.

Auriel swims right in.

The moment his head touches the magma, there's an explosion of light, light that is also liquid as it blooms from the boa constrictor's body. Then the body itself bursts and explodes, all the light that it contained blasting out into the water.

Auriel is gone.

Rumi's dazzled by the sudden illumination, is still reeling from the brightness of it when the first shock wave reaches him. As it does, his eardrums fill with a booming noise, and the force of the water surge knocks him against the cavern wall. His bones creak, and he tastes blood in his mouth. As he kicks out in the darkness, the stones around him rumble and shatter, deafening him and buffeting his body with powerful currents. It's impossible to know which way to go, how to avoid being pushed farther below to drown, how to avoid the invisible shivering boulders plummeting all around.

As Rumi flails in the water, he glimpses an orange-yellow light. His impulse is to head toward it, toward sunshine. As he makes his first stroke in its direction, though, he realizes that it's not daylight he's seeing; it's the last of Auriel's explosion. It's exactly where he should *not* be going. He reverses course.

New waves of hot ashy water push against Rumi, searing his skin even as they fill his senses with rocks and soil. At least these painful currents are pushing him away from the blast. He rockets along the passageway that he used to reach the underground cavern, right up the chasm and through the next passageway, pinging off the walls and ceiling, trying to stay alert and conscious despite the many blows to his head.

Rumi's world is only dark roaring, and he loses all orientation. He rockets down a side passage that narrows suddenly, until—*thup!*—Rumi is wedged tight. He struggles to free himself, but there isn't enough strength in his tiny arms and legs. More hot water from the explosion pushes against his legs, scalding them. The pressure is greater and greater, the agony making Rumi cry out into the dark water of the ocean depths. It's not just his flaying skin; his muscles and bones are squeezed by the pressure . . . until suddenly Rumi shoots free, zooming forward. There's no directing where he goes, not at this speed. He scrunches his eyes shut, puts his arms over his head, and hopes he doesn't wind up splattered against a rock wall or impaled on a sharp outcropping.

Instead, he can feel the current slowing, the water around him chilling. Rumi opens his eyes again, and reaches out his arms and legs, trying to feel what's nearby, where he might be in the system of caves.

It's impossible. He's not in a cave. He's swimming in wide-open pitch-black water.

Rumi shivers uncontrollably. Is this the end? There's no point swimming in any one direction, not when he might be bringing himself even farther from safety.

"Hello?" he croaks in the water, using his air magic to amplify the sound. "Hello?"

Only darkness and silence in reply.

"Hello?" he tries again.

A shift in the black. It ripples.

Rumi squints.

In the center of the ripple, an arrow of flame holds steady in the dark.

Gogi! The air bubble must be back.

"I'm coming, I'm coming!" Rumi chirps as he strokes his cramping legs through the water.

The orange arrow nears and nears until . . . *plop*.

Rumi passes through the membrane of the air bubble, bouncing twice on the ground before he comes to rest on his back, gasping for air.

Three beautiful faces above him: a monkey, a sloth, a macaw. "Oh my gosh," Rumi manages to say. He wants to make words, but can't get his brain to form them. *I am so glad to see you three. I was worried I wouldn't, that I wouldn't be able to say good-bye.*

"We're glad to see you too!" Gogi says, as if reading his thoughts. "When we heard you slipping down, and then Auriel disappeared, we had no idea if you were okay, or if you were even still alive." Tears run down his furry cheeks, already wet with seawater.

Rumi manages to get his muscles to coordinate well enough to sit himself up. "Auriel!" he gasps.

"What about Auriel?" Sky asks.

"Sacrifice . . . boom," Rumi sputters, for once at a loss for any big words.

"Um . . . guys?" Banu says.

"Auriel is dead?" Sky asks, feathers drooping.

"Yes," Rumi says.

Sky blinks his eyes heavily, the feathers on top of his head going flat.

"Sacrificed himself . . . saved us . . . made explosion . . . against magma," Rumi manages.

"Guys," Banu presses.

"Oh my gosh," Gogi says to Rumi, rocking on his heels. "Auriel has been trying to get to this moment, fought to rush us underwater, all because he meant to sacrifice himself. I think this was his plan all along."

"*Guys!*" Banu says, raising his voice for the first time Rumi has ever heard. "Would you take a look at that?"

Rumi follows Banu's gaze. Through the expanse of black water, he spies a chaotic jumble of stone and boiling water, all backlit by the orange lava beyond. "That's where Auriel plugged the magma flow," Rumi says.

"Yes . . . but look what's . . . happening to it."

Now Rumi sees what's gotten Banu's attention. The magma is mounting up behind the blockade.

Auriel's fix won't last for long.

"One implosion isn't enough to stop the force of all that magma," Sky says. "We shouldn't have gotten our hopes up. The pressure has to be even higher than ever."

"Maybe we should make a run for it," Gogi says, his voice squeaking off at the end.

"More pressure than ever," Rumi says, tapping his lips. "More pressure than ever."

"Yes. So let's make a run for it," Banu says.

"Hold on," Sky says. "What are you thinking, Rumi? Hurry! We only have a few seconds."

"More pressure than ever . . ." Rumi repeats.

His mind goes to the fish egg he saw in the pictures back in the Cave of Riddles. How it bulged out everywhere, until the two-legs lanced it.

Back then, it had seemed like a portrait of cruelty. But maybe, maybe—

"It was a message!" Rumi shrieks.

"Okay, super, you can tell us all about it later," Gogi says.

"Auriel plugged the one hole that was right under Caldera. But that's only the first step," Rumi says quickly.

Sky swings his head back and lets out a loud caw. "We have to release the magma a safe distance away from the rainforest, before it comes back out here!" he exclaims.

"The place marked with the X on the tunnel map," Rumi says.

"Can you lead us there?" Sky asks.

Rumi nods. "It was one and a half frog-lengths into the tunnel on the map, which could calibrate to maybe a thousand frog-lengths back along the real live tunnel."

"Enough talking, more doing!" Gogi says frantically, his eyes on the intensifying magma glow.

"Hold on!" Rumi cries. He chirps for joy. Finally he

doesn't have to think about what's the right course. He just knows it, feels it deep in his bones.

Rumi opens his mouth.

He lets out the biggest stream of wind he's ever made.

## 20

RUMI PROJECTILES RIGHT into Banu, pushing the sloth back down the tunnel. Sky and Gogi—and the protective bubble—tumble along with them. As they hurtle along, Rumi does quick calculations in his mind, using proportions and his memory of the two-legs' carving to decide where there will still be volcanic magma below them, but only open water above instead of rainforest.

The orange glow of Auriel's blockage is too far away to see now. He'll have to imagine what's happening, whether the pressure of the magma has already become enough to burst through. *A little more, a little more*, Rumi thinks. Then he shuts his mouth, so they slow to a stop.

*This should be about right.*

"Okay," Rumi says. "Here we go."

"Here we go what?" Gogi asks, holding his belly. All this jet travel must be giving him motion sickness.

Sky's a step ahead, though. "A little fire-wind-water flurry?" he asks, looking downward.

"You got it!" Rumi says. "I'll lead with the air. Banu and Gogi, add your elements once you can. As much as possible, so we can drill down deep. Once we hit magma, we need to get out of here as quickly as possible." Even their fastest might not be fast enough, not once the ocean water surrounding them boils.

He can't give them any more warnings, though, because his mouth is needed for other things. Planting himself firmly in Gogi's armpit, Rumi directs a needle-thin blast of air into the rock floor of the tunnel. He rises—and Gogi with him. Rumi can hear wing beats as Sky hops to Gogi's head and flaps, forcing the monkey to stay on the ground.

"Oh . . ." Banu says. "I get what we're doing now." He adds water to Rumi's air drill.

"Ooh, pretty," Gogi says, the water sizzling into steam as he mixes in his fire. The drill of water and air lights up in yellows, then reds, then—with a grunt of exertion from Gogi—blues. Outside of the hottest core of the drill, all is steam and bits of rock shrapnel.

"I think it's working!" Sky caws from above.

Rumi can't afford to say anything in response, not if he wants to keep up the drill's stream. He listens to the surging ocean all around him, the whine of splintering rock, the roar of water turning to steam. Waves of hot water wash against him; bits of disintegrated stone abrade his skin.

"Oh, I see it, I see it!" Sky says. "Stop the drill!"

Rumi shuts his mouth and looks down to witness a wall of frothy boiling seawater bearing up on them, lit in orange from the lava released beneath. "Oh no," is all he manages to say before the wall of water strikes.

It's upon them. Banu's sphere of air vanishes. Rumi loses track of his friends as he rolls and tumbles, the water scalding him then freezing him then scalding him again as he bashes against rocks and sand and shells. There's something sharp against his chin, and at first he assumes he's hit a spike of rock or shell. But then the sharp thing vanishes, and the water turns warm and almost sweet. He realizes that he's been plucked out of the ocean by Sky. That he's inside Sky's mouth.

*Eww?* Mostly *phew.*

Rumi grips the macaw's rough black tongue. Sure, maybe it would be a little gross under any other circumstance, but right now being inside Sky's mouth is saving Rumi's life, so it's A-okay by him.

They roll and pitch, Rumi flying around Sky's mouth while the explosion's watery blasts buffet him. Keeping his arms around Sky's tongue, the tree frog presses his feet against the roof of Sky's mouth, in case his friend swallows by accident.

Sky must have hit a current, as Rumi's pushed flat against the back of the macaw's throat. He can only imagine what the blasts are doing to his friends, without a bird skull around them for protection. It's impossible to know what's happening on the outside of Sky. It's impossible to know whether the macaw is still alive, Rumi is startled to realize.

Sky slows his forward movement. Have they made it out of the tunnel, and back into open water? Rumi props himself up as best as he can, waiting for the next bone-thudding propulsion. Instead they're rising, gently rising. Rumi can't imagine Sky swimming, but perhaps Banu is raising them with his bubble—or Sky's dead body is floating to the surface.

But no, Sky is definitely alive. The macaw's tongue vibrates as his muscles reengage, as the bones joining his wings to his rib cage shudder and pull. Rumi is lifted up and down in a soft rhythm. They're flying. The soft movement continues, until Rumi's stomach lurches, and he knows they've started to descend.

A slam and a shake, and then Sky's skidding along

the ground. A few steps, then the bird tumbles to his side, and his mouth parts.

Dizzy and gasping for air, Rumi picks his way out of the open beak.

Hot sand beneath his hands and feet. He cursed this beach before, how it burned his soft, porous skin, but now he feels like he could lie there for hours, soaking in the heat. His cold blood warms enough that he can finally think straight. "Sky, thank you, thank you," Rumi says, rolling over to look at his friend. "You saved my life. I'd be dead without you . . . Sky?" Rumi props himself up on an elbow. "Are you okay?"

The scarlet macaw is on his side, beak open, vacant eye staring into the open sky. Rumi hops nearer. "Sky? Answer me! What's going on with you?"

Once he's close, he can see Sky's tongue twitch, can feel the slightest hint of breath. But there's white foam around that tongue, and there's froth at the corner of Sky's beak.

*Poison.*

Rumi's stomach drops. He's poisoned his best friend.

"Oh no, no no," Rumi says, slapping Sky's feathery cheek. "Sky. I was worked up by the explosion, I didn't mean to envenomate, I'm sorry, I'm so sorry!"

Rumi looks around the beach desperately. In the distance he can see the makeshift escape craft, the tapirs standing at the shore and staring out into the sea. They can't see him, though—and what could they do to help if they could? Still, Rumi hops into the air and waves his little arms, using his magic to project his voice. "Help! Help us!"

Sobbing, he wraps his hands around Sky's neck. "I'm so sorry, my friend. I'm so sorry!"

A voice comes from the tree line. "Move, Rumi, move!"

He snaps his head up to see a panther streaking toward him—Mez! "Rumi, get out of the way!"

"I poisoned him," Rumi wails. "I didn't mean to, it just happened. I've done it again."

"Get out of the way, Rumi!" Mez shrieks.

Now Rumi sees why. Lima is tucked under Mez's chin. The bat springs into the air as they get close, immediately zooming to Sky's beak.

"I've never treated poison before," Lima squeaks. "I don't know how to start."

"Just do something!" Rumi says. "Anything. Please, Lima, please help."

"On it," she says. "Mez, keep Sky's beak pried open."

Mez pulls Sky's beak apart with a front and back paw, muscles straining with the effort. On her back, Lima inches into his mouth. "Ugh, parrot breath is the worst. Oh yes, I see some tissue damage in here, wow, more than some, hold on. . . ."

A few moments later, she's back out. "I licked what I could in there, but I assume the poison is in his blood-stream now. I don't know what to do next—I mean, I can't get inside Sky."

"Maybe not," Rumi says. "But you could get in contact with his bloodstream."

"How's that?" Lima asks quizzically, head cocked. A glob of parrot slobber dangles from her ear.

After quickly checking his hands to make sure they're no longer envenomated, Rumi parts the feathers along Sky's thigh. His friend's flesh already feels like it's cooling. "Mez, I need you to slit the skin here."

She doesn't need to be asked twice. Mez extracts one claw and makes a single clean slice between the parted red feathers, down the white flesh of Sky's leg. Blood wells up, more crimson than Sky's feathers, made even more shockingly bright by the harsh midday sun.

"Now what?" Lima asks, looking down apprehensively.

"Drop a little saliva in," Rumi says.

"You mean spit into his cut?"

"Yes, I mean spit into his cut."

Lima makes a hawking sound, and then she spits right into Sky's wound, coating it in bat saliva. Rumi is amazed to see Sky's wound seal together right in front of his eyes, the saliva trapped inside . . . hopefully in the macaw's bloodstream.

He hops so he's in front of Sky's closed eye. Mez releases his beak so it half closes. Rumi can't tell whether Sky's still breathing, not with the hot air rising from the sand of the beach. There's no motion under Sky's eyes, and his claws are drawn up tight. They curl, like a dead bird's.

*Like a dead bird's.*

"Oh, Sky," Rumi wails, hurling his head into his palms, so all he can see is his own moist amphibian skin. "I'm sorry. There was so much we still needed to explore together, and I . . . I . . . *killed* you."

Sky's body shudders. His crimson feathers lift and lower, rippling in a wave from his claws to the top of his head.

"Well, that's an overstatement," Sky rasps.

Rumi looks up, vision murky with tears. "What?"

"I might not be feeling so hot," the macaw says, "but I'm pretty sure I'm alive."

Lima claps her wings, and Mez cheers, but Rumi can't take his eyes off his friend, brought back to life right here in front of him. Rumi hurls himself around the soggy flight feathers of Sky's neck, breathes in their musty scent. "You're okay, you're okay," he finally manages to say. "I can't believe it."

"That's enough," Sky says. "I'm not quite ready to hug all of this out. I'm in a bad mood. You did nearly kill me, after all."

Rumi hops away. "Sorry, I get it."

Sky scrunches his eyes shut and then opens them. "That was supposed to be a joke."

Sky flaps his wings and extends his claws, but when he tries to get up, he just flops to his side. He manages to tilt his head so he can see Lima. "I can sense your magic in my bloodstream. Thank you, my friend."

Lima squeaks. "Did you just call me 'friend'?"

Sky's eye opens wide. "Have I never said that before?"

Lima shakes her head.

"Oh," Sky says. "I'm sure I meant to."

Lima reaches out a wingtip and pokes Sky, as if testing to see if he's still real.

Mez's ears go flat. "Now that that emergency is over, we need to talk," she says. "What happened down there?"

A thought strikes Rumi, and the moment it does, sudden panic sends him hopping into the air. "Where are Gogi and Banu? We got separated."

Mez points down the beach, where the emergency escape raft is just visible on the horizon. "Lima and I passed them on our way in. They're a little waterlogged, and Gogi's complaining to no end, but they'll be fine. Their air bubble popped out of the sea, and Zuza and the other tapirs mounted a rescue to bring them to shore. Banu's magic kept them alive. We'd been waiting for you—we got here last night after dealing with Mist. Chumba's the new leader of the panther family, by the way—"

"Yes!" Rumi exclaims. "I was watching."

"Right, of course. Anyway, I just got finished fishing Gogi and Banu out of the water, and that's—"

"I helped too!" Lima says.

"Lima helped, too. That's when we heard you yelling, so we made our way right over here."

Rumi shakes his head. "We have a *lot* to catch up on."

"Yes," Mez says. "So, are we all safe now?"

"I don't know," Rumi says. He looks toward the horizon. There's still a tendril of smoke rising from the volcano at the rainforest's center . . . but the tendril is much smaller than the plumes that had once been spewing out into the sky. He thinks about Auriel's dogged pursuit of the tunnels and chasms that led to the magma core, of his disappearing in a blaze of light and energy, of the collapse of the chasm where the hot lava had been rising, of opening the new release vent, far from land. He can see a geyser of water off at the horizon, sending sprays of steam high into the air.

Rumi lets out a deep breath. "I think . . . I think we are. I think we're safe."

THEY SET UP camp at the edge of the beach. Tapirs crush a lot of vegetation when they circle to make their beds, and they've generated enough flattened greenery to make a soft surface for all the shadowwalkers to sleep in. The friends huddle down in the center of a ring of softly dozing herbivores. Mez and Gogi are on the grass, Lima dozing on top of Banu's butt while Rumi lounges in a freshwater puddle. Sky usually takes up a position on the edge of camp, but this time he's right in the middle of everyone, looking mighty grateful indeed for his friends.

"Sleeping in the middle of a ring of tapirs is the way to *do* it," Gogi says, lying back with his hands behind his head. "This is the best rest I've had in a long time."

"I'm glad too," Mez says. "Sky, especially, needs a safe place to recover."

"He saved my life," Rumi says. He's been used to being in control of his feelings, but now they feel like they're gushing around him, like mud under a foot. "I would have been squished flat by that surge of water. Sky didn't even think twice about taking me into his mouth, even though it was nearly the death of him. I'm lucky to have him as my best friend."

"To think he used to be enemy number one," Mez says.

"Well, I'd say Auriel was enemy number one in those days," Lima corrects, "even if we didn't totally know it yet. Sky was enemy number two."

"And yet Auriel made good," Rumi says. "He learned after his betrayal by the Ant Queen. It's almost like his desire to redeem himself was what was animating him after death, and now he's finally been released from his duty."

"That's a cheerful way . . . of looking at it," Banu says, shrugging. It's a sloth shrug, so it takes a while.

"Maybe no one's a forever enemy," Rumi postulates, wriggling into the cool nighttime sand. This salt-free water is doing wonders at getting the sting out of his layers of skin. That, and a quick once-over with Lima saliva. "Maybe it's all about context."

"Except in the case of Mist," Mez says darkly.

Lima nods. "Except Mist. We gave him about five chances too many."

"I'm sorry, Mez," Rumi says. "It must have been so hard to witness what he's done to the rest of your family. Then to have to fight him as well!"

"I'm not going to let him hurt me or my family anymore," Mez says. "I'm sealing him off in my mind. I'm never going to think about him again."

"You can *do* that?" Lima asks, amazed.

A self-mocking smile curls Mez's lip away from her teeth. "No. But that doesn't mean I can't *try*."

"It's not so easy, keeping your mind off the ones who've hurt you," Sky says.

Rumi startles and looks at his friend. He'd thought Sky was asleep. The macaw is still too weak to fly, but at least his breathing is deep and regular. Rumi picks his way out of the freshwater puddle and climbs onto Sky's back. "Maybe we can help you heal that way, too."

Sky's feathers bristle and then relax. "Maybe you can. I had a rough start, but my feelings about being abandoned by my parents get more distant with every day. Thanks to you all."

"Sort of like the volcano," Rumi says, sitting up and looking toward the center of the rainforest. "It seems to have quieted down now that it's found the right release."

"I'm most definitely glad about that," Mez says, a yawn exposing her long, sharp teeth to the night air.

"Yes, I think we'd all rather not have our rainforest go up in smoke," Gogi says.

"Once we're sure we don't need the escape craft, I'm going to head back to my home jungle," Mez says. "There's a lot of work to do to restore the natural order there, and I don't want Chumba to have to go it alone."

"I'll come with you," Lima says. "I love hanging out with panthers."

"And the rest of you?" Mez asks. "Will you join us?"

"I've been thinking about Auriel's sacrifice," Rumi says. "For every enemy that makes good, there will be new ones that crop up. I'm thinking we should create an order that keeps an eye on the whole rainforest, investigating trouble as it comes up. The Protectors of Caldera, we could call it."

"Ooh. I like the ring of that," Gogi says, nodding.

"We all exist in solitude," Sky says. "I think it would be smart for the animals to be in better communication. I can use my magical abilities to help connect everyone. To stop other animals from having to struggle alone, like we all once did."

"The Protectors of Caldera," Lima says, weighing the words. "Ooh, what else could we call ourselves?

Rainforest Squad. No, no . . . Shadowwalker Force. No, no, I got it! The Watchers of Caldera."

"Nice, Lima," Gogi says, giving her a high five. Or a high "one," since Lima's fingertips are spread along her wing.

"Who's in?" Rumi asks.

Banu extends a claw. "Count me in."

Two wings, a paw, and two hands join. "It starts now!" Gogi says.

"Ooh," Lima says, wriggling. "That moment just gave me the shivers."

"We can use the panther forest as a home base," Mez says excitedly. "And we can recruit other animals from around the rainforest to join our ranks."

"It depends," Gogi says. "Is Chumba going to be a nice queen?"

"The very best," Mez says.

"I figured as much," Gogi says. "Maybe we can pick up Alzo on the way. I miss that guy."

"Travel to the panther rainforest will take us near the ziggurat ruins, where the lava was threatening to erupt," Rumi says. "We can confirm once and for all that this danger is past us."

Sky nods—or tries to nod. In his weakened state it's more like a heavy wink followed by a beak clack. "That's wise."

Banu yawns. "You all go ahead . . . I'm going to rest around here . . . for a while . . . I'll catch up . . . I know where . . . the panther forest is."

Rumi nods. "Your help was invaluable. We'd all be dead without you."

"I'm very glad . . . that you're . . . not all dead."

Gogi ruffles Banu's hair. "Aww, that's sweet, buddy."

"I'm glad about that too!" Lima squeaks. She gets to work smoothing her wings over Banu's head. "Banu looks much better with his hair parted the other way. Well, he looks super handsome either way, to be honest."

Banu peers up at his two stylists, eyes wide. "I've never really thought . . . about my hairstyle . . . thank you."

Mez stares at them incredulously, as if wondering how Caldera could have ever possibly been saved by the likes of them. She lets out a low whistle. "Ooookay. Should we get started?"

"Yep, first thing after the Veil rises," Gogi says, stretching out his long, furry body.

"No. Now," Mez says, looking up at the dark new-moon sky. "I want to start back toward Chumba *now*."

Gogi cracks his knuckles. "I should have known you were going to say something like that."

"It's wise to travel by night, and there's nothing keeping us on this beach anymore," Rumi says, nodding.

"Night flying is the best. But I don't think Sky can even stand right now," Lima points out.

Sky scrunches his eyes shut, flutters his wings once, twice, then rises into the air. He soars up to a branch and lands there, unsteady at first, but then poised and unmoving. "I'm good, don't worry about me," he caws.

"Wow," Gogi says. "Just a moment ago, you were totally stricken. How do you do that?"

"Willpower, my friend," Sky says, winking.

"Yep. That was never a strong suit of mine."

"Okay, everyone," Mez says. "Let's go."

22

AS THEY TRAVEL inland, Rumi becomes more and more convinced that Caldera will recover from its near miss with destruction. The volcanic smoke has mostly disappeared. There's still a charred scent to the air, still a haze to the distant horizon, but the day skies right overhead are clear and blue, the night skies black and untinged by the red glow that was once at the horizon. The shadowwalkers' frantic plan—and the long-ago work of the two-legs, when they built that tunnel for their hunched wheeled creatures, and then carved their cryptic advice—prevented disaster.

"Hey, can we pass by the ziggurat while we're on our

way to the panther forest?" Gogi asks. "It might be nice to stroll down memory lane."

"It will cost us zero point seven extra days," Rumi replies, "but if Mez is okay with the delay, I'd like the opportunity to examine the old ziggurat carvings again."

"We'll see," Mez says as she picks her way over a particularly muscular liana vine. "We've only just started. We have a long time yet before we're near Caldera's center."

"I'd vote for visiting the ziggurat too," Sky says, his voice still weak from his brush with death. "It's fitting, I think, to visit the place where Caldera's worries began, now that they're over."

"Let's not speak too soon," Mez warns, eyes scanning the jungle.

Rumi nods at Sky. "I remember when we all first came together. We were so nervous and suspicious of one another."

"Yeah, I'm pretty sure Mez peed her fur when she first arrived," Lima says.

"I did *not*!"

"I miss Niko the catfish," Lima says. "It must have been so hard for him, a fish around so many land creatures. I was impressed he even made it to the ziggurat." She pauses, thinking. "And getting his bones crunched by Auriel, until he died. That must have been hard for him too."

"He might have bonded with the grouper we met under the sea," Rumi says. "I really will go find it after this is all over."

"You always were true to your word," Sky says. "We're lucky to have you among the Protectors of Caldera."

"Nah, I've decided we should go with Rainforest Squad," Lima announces.

"Anyway," Gogi says, yawning and stretching his arms over his head. "The ziggurat is far away still, and we don't want to overexert ourselves. How about a power nap before we—whoa!"

Mez lets out a high-pitched squeal as Gogi leaps into a thicket. "What are you doing?" Rumi asks, but then he sees what set Gogi's reflexes firing.

The very leaves of the trees themselves have become sharp teeth, ferocious sharp teeth—

Mist has Mez's neck in his mouth.

Mist has pounced right into their midst.

Mez is trapped in his jaws.

Blood trickles down calico fur as Mist crunches down.

"No, no!" Rumi tries to cry, but his voice won't make a sound, the shock is too great, he can do nothing but stare at Mist with Mez in his mouth.

How can this be happening?

Is this a dream?

Rumi realizes it's not, it's definitely not, when Gogi hurls a fan of fire at Mist's tail, setting the white fur ablaze. Mist yelps and rolls away, and instantly Mez whirls to the attack, claws out and jaws open. As Mist skulks away, slapping his smoldering tail against the ground as he goes, Mez leaps on him. Her cousin is slowed by his awkward position, and she's able to lunge onto his back, teeth locked around his neck. In a moment, the ambush has turned.

Rumi sends out a blast of air, but he can't get a direct hit on Mist without striking Mez too, so he can only watch, mouth agape, as Mez and Mist go tumbling. They're a blur of white and calico, leaves and dirt flying.

Gogi's the first to mobilize, racing toward the combatants. He skids to a stop. It's not until Rumi's hops have allowed him to catch up that the frog can see why Gogi has held still.

Mez is on top of Mist, pinning him on his back. They've rolled over Sky in the process, and he lies off to one side, motionless. Mez howls as she prepares to make the fatal bite. "You followed us," Mez says. "You tailed us and waited for the moment to sneak attack. You could have joined us at any time, but you didn't. You would have burned up with the rainforest, but we saved you—and then you ambush me from out of nowhere."

Mist struggles to break free, but Mez is too strong. "Of course I couldn't let you defeat me and not try for revenge," he spits. "I'd sooner die."

"That you will. This is the last time you betray us, cousin," Mez says. "I'm all out of forgiveness. Now I only ask that you forgive me for what I'm about to do."

After one agonized yowl, she clamps her teeth around Mist's throat. He flails, using his last energy to try to get free, but he can't. Beneath Mez's ferocious grip, he seems beyond even using his magic. Finally he goes motionless, his head lolling to one side.

Still Mez doesn't release him. She thrashes, the muscles of her jaws clenching tight. It's too gruesome; Rumi has to look away.

"Shh, Mez, it's over," Gogi says. Rumi allows himself to look, and sees Gogi with his hand on Mez's haunch. She's released her cousin's still body and is panting with exhaustion, her eyes closed.

Lima's next to Sky, helping him up. "Sky will live!" she says. "He got clawed a bit when the panthers rolled over him, but it's not too deep. I don't think he will even need any healing magic."

Sky caws weakly. "I'll take some anyway, if you're offering."

Rumi hops over to take a good look at Mist's motion-less body. "You did all you could, Mez. You gave him every chance."

She nods. "I promised myself I would put a final stop to him if he attacked again. That I wouldn't give him another chance to hurt the ones I love. But still, I hoped I wouldn't have to kill my own cousin."

Mez is interrupted by eerie laughter. "No, it can't be," she sputters, springing to all fours.

Rumi's brain struggles to catch up: Mist's body is not dead. Mist's body is laughing. *Mist* is not dead. Mist is . . . still alive!

Mist continues his chilling laughter as he sits up. He's bloodied around his neck, but otherwise he seems . . . fine. Impossibly fine. He growls at Mez. "You've failed at every promise you made. You were banished from our family. You let the Ant Queen get away so many times. And now you can't even kill me."

Mez hisses and prepares to go back on the offensive.

"Save your energy," Mist says. "I can no longer be killed. Didn't you wonder why the nightwalker cult wor-shipped me as a god? Because I *am* one, cousin. I'm immortal."

"But . . . how?" Gogi asks.

"The lunar eclipse released the magical energies that resided in the Ant Queen," Rumi says as the horrible truth dawns on him. "The two-legs imprisoned her because she couldn't be killed. Just like he received some of our magic, Mist must have also received the Ant Queen's power to live forever."

Mist laughs again. It's a hollow, self-mocking sound, the unhappiest laughter Rumi has ever heard. "You should listen to your little frog friend, Mez," Mist says. "You'll never be rid of me."

Mez's ears go flat, her whiskers pull alongside her cheeks, and she closes her eyes.

When she opens them, though, there's a fiery resolve in her eyes. "Maybe you're right, and I'll never be rid of you. But Caldera will be."

Rumi's eyes go wide. What does *that* mean?

"First," Mez says shrewdly, staring Mist down with flat ears and bared teeth, "we have to subdue you."

Though he's not sure what Mez has planned, Rumi takes a hop toward Mist. The white panther's brows rise. "What do you think you're going to do, tree frog? Kill me with breezes?"

"Why, you big—" Gogi starts to say, flames licking on his palms.

"No, Gogi," Rumi says. "Let me take care of this."

He opens his mouth. He closes his mouth. Time to try out the full new extent of his magic.

Rumi lifts his hands up to the sky. Mist watches him, confused.

There's no holding back, not anymore. That nagging guilty voice that tormented him for so long has disappeared.

"See you on the other side," Rumi says.

He brings his hands down.

With them comes a concentrated wind, a cylinder of gale, a column of cyclone. It smacks Mist right on the top of his head and sends him sprawling on the earth. He rolls to a stop, his tongue lolling.

The wind holds for a moment, flattening Mist's white fur, then it dissipates.

Rumi hops over and listens for breathing. "He's unconscious," he reports, satisfied. "Wow. That worked even better than I hoped. And if he acts up again, I'll smash him with another column of air."

Rumi waits for an answer. "Did you all hear me?"

He looks over to see his friends staring at him slack-jawed, dumbfounded in amazement. Their wind-mussed hair and feathers stick out in all directions, making them all look a little crazy.

"Nifty, huh?" Rumi asks.

"Rumi," Gogi says, hands over his mouth. "That. Was. Amazing."

SUNLIGHT STREAMING ALL around, Zuza shoulders open the rigid bands girding the ark and presents the cool, dark inside to the shadowwalkers. Rumi hops in, revived by the chilly air. It smells of the insides of trees: bracing, crisp, slightly minty. "It's lovely in here, guys!" he calls. "Come on in!"

As his eyes adjust, he sees that the interior of the ark is elegantly banded in thin reeds, broad banana leaves, and a layer of mud that's hardened to become a sort of plaster. Rumi gives it an experimental rap. Firm and unflaking—it just might hold up against the conditions of the open sea.

Beak over claw, Sky picks his way through the

opening and pauses, silhouetted by the sunlight behind him. He inspects the walls, floor, and ceiling closely before giving a nod of approval. "It's like a really clean cave in here."

"THAT'S JUST WHAT I WAS THINKING!"

Rumi and Sky shriek and go scrambling, only slowing when Lima flits down from the ceiling. "Sorry, did I surprise you? I spent the morning in here, because it's so cool and dark. It really feels like the best bat cave I could imagine. I made myself right at home."

Heart rate finally returning to normal, Rumi taps a puddle of bat guano with two fingers, the only blemish on the ark's clean floor. "Yes, I noticed."

"Hey, dropping guano is a sign of respect and hospitality in bat culture," Lima sniffs. "It's good luck for our coming voyage."

"Yeah, poop plays a very important part in both our societies," Gogi says reverentially as he enters the ark. He's moving slower than usual, as his arms are full of supplies. He drops them in a heap on the ark floor, then rubs his aching biceps. Rumi knows that the leaf-wrapped bundles contain nuts, fruits, greens, even a mass of delicious water bugs they skimmed off the surface of a nearby pond—enough supplies to keep them fed for a long trip.

"It's so dark and cramped in here," Gogi says,

frowning. It appears monkeys have their own tastes in ark accommodations.

Rumi lays a reassuring hand on his friend's tail. "Sky, show him the trick you managed."

"Yes, check it out," Sky says. He bows his head and ruffles out his tail feathers.

"Is that . . . it?" Gogi asks. "That's, um, super cool, Sky."

"No," Rumi whispers. "Just wait."

The ceiling of the ark glimmers and then fades, to display the beach all around them, the calm blue ocean waves to one side. It's like the whole top half of the ark has been removed—but when Gogi lifts his arms, they still strike the ceiling. "Oh, wow, you've come a long way in your visions, Sky," he says. "We're contained and dry, but still have a great view. Best of both worlds!"

"Precisely!" Rumi says.

"I embedded a few feathers into the woven fibers on the outside of the ark," Sky explains, opening his eyes. "Since the directives are this close, it's even easier to channel them. I can move around and talk and not break the image."

"This is going to be amazing," Lima says. "I hope this trip takes forever."

"I don't," Mez says as she appears in the entrance. She's backing in, dragging something large behind her.

Once she clears the lip of the craft, she tumbles into the pile of leaf-wrapped food supplies.

Mist tumbles after her. He's in full daycoma, but even so they've bound his limbs with strong liana vine. None of them wants to risk having a powerful enemy out and about an enclosed vessel.

"I can't even stand to look at him," Gogi says, turning his back on their captive.

"I'd recommend you get over that," Mez says. "If there's anything I've learned about Mist, it's that he'll need watching until we're finally rid of him."

A sloth's head peers in the opening, next to Zuza's sweet, questioning eyes. "Are you guys . . . all ready to go?" Banu asks.

"Yep!" Lima says. "I still wish you were coming with us."

"I wish . . . I could," he says. "But I've definitely . . . overextended myself." With that, he topples over to one side on the beach, snoring away.

"Don't worry, everyone," Zuza says. "We tapirs will take good care of him until you're back. He deserves some pampering."

Rumi looks around at his friends, hands on his frog hips. "Are we ready, everyone? Any final doubts or questions?"

"Nope," Gogi says. Together with Mez, he rolls

Mist's comatose body until he splashes into the container they've fashioned for him—they've tied up a broad banana leaf to make a bowl, and filled it with seawater. Mist will be traveling up to his chin in liquid, just in case he tries any fire tricks. Not that they expect him to, after Rumi's column of air knocked him out.

Rumi lets his gaze linger on Mez, whose ears are flat against her head. She clearly can't be rid of Mist soon enough.

Zuza closes the door to the ark with a thud. Gogi uses the vines on the inside to bind it shut.

"Find something to hold on to, everyone!" Rumi calls as he moves toward the rear of the craft.

Gogi looks around the ark's smooth surface, scratching an armpit. "Um, Rumi, there *isn't* anything to hold on to."

"Oops. Well, I guess just brace yourselves, then!"

Rumi presses his fingers against the wall of the craft, then generates wind on the opposite side. It's the latest trick he's managed with his magic. Ever since he got his big secret off his chest, he's been able to play loose with his power, even detaching the wind source from his body itself. He watches through Sky's image of the outside as the sand of the beach kicks up a zephyr. Zuza faces away, shielding Banu with her body.

The ark begins to tip and rock, then skates down the beach. Rumi hears his companions scrambling in the ark, but focuses on the wind, shifting it as needed to keep the craft headed toward the ocean.

Then—*splash*—they're floating on the water. The ark moves much faster now, and Rumi's same volume of wind sends it shooting and skimming across the waves. "Woo, woo!" Lima cheers.

Rumi lets the wind relax so they're moving at a calmer pace. He turns to see his friends jumbled in the middle of the ark, a big pile of indistinguishable paws and noses and wings and claws and tails. "Is everyone okay?"

Lima pops out of the huddle, clapping her wings. "That was awesome!"

Gogi looks less thrilled as he picks himself out of the pile. In fact, he looks a little green. "Is it going to rock like this the whole way?" he asks, his hand braced against the side of the hull.

"I think that's probably unavoidable," Sky says as he pops out from under Mez's legs. "Believe me, I'm not feeling so good about it, either."

Mez has all four legs spread wide, tail thrashing as she sways from side to side. "Maybe we'll get used to it?"

"I think you will," Rumi says. He pauses. "Hopefully you will."

It's not too long before the shadowwalkers have arranged their foodstuffs back into neat piles and made sure Mist is secure in his watery restraints. Mez sits at the front of the craft, peering out at the horizon, newly calm—if a little ill-looking. Gogi sits next to her, draping an arm across her shoulders and a tail across her haunches. That extra limb makes him an especially good comforter. "We'll sight another land soon, I'm sure of it," he says.

"And then we'll set Mist up and skedaddle out of there," Lima says, taking up her recent favorite spot, upside down under Mez's chin. "Operation Immortal Exile is going to be a success."

"Maybe we could explore any new land we find a little bit first, though?" Rumi asks. "This could be our one chance to get to know someplace that isn't Caldera. I wouldn't want to waste that opportunity."

"I second that," Sky says. "Who knows what we might discover out there?"

"We *will* come home eventually, right?" Gogi asks. "Alzo would kill me if I left Caldera without saying good-bye."

"Yes," Rumi says emphatically. "We'll banish Mist somewhere, and then we'll come home."

They draw quiet as they gaze out at the sunstruck ocean. The watery light casts glowing interlocking lines across the walls and floor of the ark, like Banu's bubble did when they were walking along the bottom of the sea.

Rumi taps the wrapped leaf bundle closest to him and, making sure no one is looking, delicately unfolds a corner and peers in. There they are—three little green growths, each with a clod of soil to keep it moist and alive. If it comes down to it, they can plant them in their new land. He's chosen representative species, at the base of every jungle ecosystem. If they have to settle somewhere that's not already rainforest, they can make it into one over time. Only if it comes to that. Ideally they'll be able to return home without needing to recreate the rainforest elsewhere. But it never hurts to be prepared.

Rumi wraps the little growths back in their protective leaf, and then hops to join his friends. He snuggles under Sky's wing, and stares out at the magically displayed expanse of sea. The skies are so bright they're almost silver. They might be the first inhabitants of Caldera ever to see another land. Who knows what they'll discover!

"Rumi," Sky says. "Look. There on the horizon. It got our message!"

"What is *that*?" Mez gasps.

A large shadow has emerged from the ocean depths. Its giant bulk turns the ocean an even darker blue, then black, and finally its fin crests the surface. The titanic fish keeps pace with the ark's bow, and then swivels to look back. "Hello there," the grouper says with its deep voice. "My name is Kay."

It smiles. Doing so causes it to reveal its giant teeth. "Gah!" Lima shrieks.

"It's our new grouper friend!" Rumi says. "Hi, Kay!"

"Kay, really?" Gogi asks. "Is that a grouper sort of name?"

"It's been a very long time since I took a journey," the grouper says. "I'm ready for an adventure."

Mez nods warily. "This is the fish friend you told us about? You hadn't mentioned it was so . . . big."

"I'll scout ahead and then check back in as the Veil drops," the grouper says. "If that treacherous friend of yours gives you any trouble whatsoever, you can send him my way."

A grim smile plays across Mez's features. "We'll be sure to. I think I'm going to like you, Kay."

"Well, well," Gogi says, cracking his knuckles. "A sturdy craft to travel in, loyal friends, magical powers, calm seas, sunny weather, a whole world to explore, and a sea monster on our side! Life is looking pretty good."

"Thanks to Auriel's sacrifice, it is," Sky says quietly.

"Yes," Gogi says, chastened. "Thanks to Auriel's sacrifice."

"I'm glad that I have you all by my side," Rumi says.

"I'm glad that we packed so many snacks," Lima says. "Lots and lots of snacks."

The friends draw quiet and close, looking out at the sun-dazzled horizon, and all that it might hold in store.

*Excerpt from*

# THE SONG OF THE FIVE

*Final Verse*

*(Translated from the original*

*Ant by Rumi Mosquitoswallow)*


*And so we ants*

*Lost our queen first and then the plan she left us.*

*With no leader to make a new plot*

*we returned to our old roles,*

*tending our nests*

*farming our aphids*

*grooming our eggs*

*With barely a thought to the doings of birds, reptiles, amphibians,*

*mammals.* ^ and Lima the Healing Bat!


*But.*

*One fledging season**

*an exhausted young ant arrived from*

*a distant land, speaking words we only just recognized*

*as Ant.*


*She spoke of five young animals who cross the Veil*

*as ants do,*

*and of their captive charge,*

*making a new home across the sea.*

---

\* Translator's note: This is when young queens grow wings and fly as far as
they can in order to form new nests.

302

*Wherever adventure happens,*
*there will always be ants*
*to sing its song.**

---

* Translator's note: Translation date changed to "Year One of New Caldera." Signing off, Rumi Mosquitoswallow. ^ and Lima the Healing Bat!

❖303❖

# ACKNOWLEDGMENTS

Books are collaborative. I couldn't have written *Rumi's Riddle* without the help of my amazing editors, Ben Rosenthal and Melissa Miller, and to everyone who's been so helpful at Katherine Tegen Books and Harper-Collins: Ro Romanello, Jackie Burke, Mabel Hsu, Tanu Srivastava, Katherine Tegen, Robby Imfeld, Megan Barlog, Meaghan Finnerty, Vaishali Nayak, Laaren Brown, Liz Byer, and many more!

Thanks as always to my agent, Richard Pine, and those who read early manuscript drafts, among them Eric Zahler, Barbara Schrefer, and Daphne Grab.